'Do you like k

'Let's just say I fe
adults.'

Keely was intrigued. 'You just don't want to get too close, right?'

Luke sat hunched over, twirling his wineglass between his palms. 'Something like that. I was an army brat, so we moved around a lot. You don't have much opportunity to make friends, and maybe that's why I'm a little wary around kids.'

'Matthew will cure you of that,' she said confidently.

'Could be that I have a missing gene or something.'

She didn't believe him. He'd been too good with Matthew, too easy. But she knew it was best to say nothing.

Draining the last of his wine, he set his glass aside. 'So now you see why I don't exactly feel qualified to play a big role in the life of any kid.'

'That's too bad.'

He was immediately suspicious. 'Why?'

'Because someone needs to play the father role for Matthew and you're the perfect man for the job.'

Dear Reader,

Welcome to the emotional, exciting world of Superromance.

This month we have two charming Christmas stories for you: *A Christmas Legacy* by Kathryn Shay, the last in the RIVERBEND books where all the mysteries and questions raised in the last four books are now finally resolved, and *What Child Is This?* by Karen Young, where a child at Christmas makes a solitary doctor aware of the joys a family could bring.

Deception from Morgan Hayes is our dramatic, action-adventure book, and *Hush, Little Baby* comes from the talented pen of Judith Arnold and is another one of those single-dads-need-a-little-help books, that make us all feel a little better about our child-rearing skills.

Enjoy!

The Editors

What Child Is This?

KAREN YOUNG

SILHOUETTE®
SUPERROMANCE™

*First published in Great Britain 2002
Silhouette Books, Eton House, 18-24 Paradise Road,
Richmond, Surrey TW9 1SR*

© Karen Stone 1999

ISBN 0 373 70881 5

38-1202

*Printed and bound in Spain
by Litografia Rosés S.A., Barcelona*

Dear Reader,

What is a Christmas story without a child? And where else is the wonder of this marvellous season more evident than when reflected in the eyes of a child?

This is not the first story I've written about displaced children and the vagaries of a system that sometimes puts kids at risk. We certainly hear a lot these days about some who go astray. So it gave me a lot of pleasure to write a story about two people who came together in love to rescue one little boy. I hope you will fall in love with Matthew, just as Luke and
Keely did.

Oh yes, and may the holiday season be a blessed and joyous one for you.

Sincerely,

Karen Young

PS I love to hear from readers. You can write to me at: PO Box 366, Jackson, MS 39205-0366, USA.

To fellow writers Linda Lewis, Joanna Wayne and
Gloria Alvarez—for help when I needed it.
Thanks, gals.

CHAPTER ONE

THE WOMAN LYING ON THE STRETCHER winced as Luke Jamison gingerly probed her rib cage, suspecting a fracture. Not a recent injury, he thought, studying the large hematoma that blossomed in angry purples, blues and muddy greens. When he pressed a spot on her abdomen, she cried out sharply. Bruised spleen, he decided, before glancing at the patient's name on the chart. "Looks like you've had a rough time lately, Mrs. Long."

"Phyllis."

"Phyllis." He turned her face into the light and frowned at a laceration near the corner of her mouth. "What happened?"

"I had a little accident in the car yesterday," the woman murmured, chewing at an already bruised lower lip. "Slammed on the brakes, then ran off into a ditch. Bumped my face on the steering wheel. That place you just touched on my belly? Well, I think it must have been the seat belt. It bruised me pretty good."

Seat belt. Yeah, right. Luke studied her battered face. The laceration could have come from a bump against a steering wheel, but no seat belt had caused the deep bruise to her spleen or the damage to her ribs. Somebody had beaten the hell out of this woman.

After motioning to Jenny Blackwell, the attending nurse, he was handed a butterfly bandage, which he carefully applied to the cut near the woman's lip. "Some of your injuries seem pretty fresh, Phyllis. Others aren't. You say the accident was yesterday?"

"Well, it was actually around midnight, and I just put off coming here."

A cut on her chin would require more than a butterfly, he thought. Probably two stitches. As Jenny lifted the sheet covering the woman, he noted that both knees were scraped. She'd probably taken a fall running from her assailant. Reaching for Betadine to cleanse the wound, he felt outrage simmering in his gut. Why was it that the holiday season brought out the beast in some people? Just a week after Thanksgiving and the "accidents" were already showing up in the E.R. Yesterday he'd treated a kid with a broken arm whose mother, in a fit of temper, had tossed him into the back seat of the car after Christmas shopping!

"And how about your knees?" Turning, he chose sterile instruments from a tray behind him. "Looks as if you might have taken a tumble. Sure you weren't running from someone?"

Phyllis turned her face away.

"I slipped and fell trying to climb out of the ditch. I was dizzy and—"

She was interrupted by the sounds of a commotion in the waiting room. Luke saw fear flare in her eyes as a man's voice rose in an angry shout. "That'd be Billy," she said, looking embarrassed. "He wanted to come in here with me but y'all wouldn't let him."

"It's hospital policy for family members to stay in the waiting room while a patient's being treated," Jenny said, passing a clean swab to Luke.

"Billy doesn't like folks ordering him around."

Jenny's laugh held no amusement. "I could have guessed that, honey." The E.R. nurse had seen hundreds of Atlanta's battered women wheeled in through St. Dominic's doors. Phyllis Long's evasions about the violence in her life didn't fool Jenny Blackwell.

"There's a good chance that two ribs are fractured," Luke told the woman. "I'm ordering an X ray."

"Oh, I don't think Billy will want to wait around for that," Phyllis said quickly. Her husband could now be heard arguing with hospital security.

"We'll insist," Luke commented dryly.

"He'll throw a fit," Phyllis warned.

"You don't have to put up with this kind of treatment," Luke said with exasperation. Didn't the woman know he was trying to help her? "You don't have to live with an abusive man. There're programs out there, Phyllis."

She looked scared but stubborn. "I told you I had a car accident."

Luke tossed the paper wrapping from the sterile sharp on the tray. "With all due respect, ma'am, your injuries tell me otherwise. The next time you might be hurt a lot worse. A blow to your head could injure your brain. Have you thought of that?" He gestured toward a bruise on her neck. "And when he's choking you, it could crush your larynx. You could die before the EMTs get to you...that is, if he decided to call for help at all."

"I don't think he'd do that," she mumbled, tucking her head. She struggled to sit up on the stretcher, while trying to hold the sheet against her chest with both hands. "Can I go now?"

"After I put in the sutures." Luke looked directly into her eyes. "Phyllis, we've got a procedure here to deal with situations like yours. All you have to do is fill out a form and sign it. We'll call the police and they'll send out someone who's had experience in this." Maybe she didn't trust him because he was a man. "It's usually a woman, right, Jenny?"

He glanced at the nurse, who wore a pained expression. Ignoring it, he said, "Go and get that form for Phyllis, will you?"

"I really want to go now." The woman was clearly anxious to escape. Wobbly but determined, she got off the stretcher and started to walk. But after two steps, she faltered, putting a hand to her head weakly.

Luke moved to help her back onto the stretcher. "Are you going to wait until you land in intensive care before you do something?" he inquired sharply.

"Please..." She bent low, covering her face with both hands.

"What's going on here?"

Luke swore beneath his breath and turned to face the icy gaze of his senior resident. One look and he knew he was in for it. Although almost ten years younger than Luke, Keely Hamilton was authoritative, vigilant and, above all, self-confident. Definitely qualities he admired in a leader, but something about them coming from Keely never failed to rub him the wrong way.

He moved into the corridor, out of earshot of his patient. "I'm treating the patient for injuries she *claims* she got in a car accident, but that jerk ranting and raving out in the waiting room is responsible for her bruises. Whatever the reason, Keely, I think I can handle it."

"Not if what I overheard was any indication, *Doctor*." Keely's tone dropped a notch, a sure sign that she was getting ready to blast him. "Can't you

see that pushing her to call in the police is coun-
terproductive? The woman's scared.''

Luke's reply was low and just as fervent. ''Better she's scared than *dead!* She's battered from
head to toe. Check out the marks on her throat, if
you don't believe me. He tried to choke her!''

Keely closed her eyes. ''And you think all it
takes to solve her problem is to browbeat her into
pressing charges? Get real, Luke. She believes that
defying him will put her in more jeopardy than
ever. She needs help, but it'll have to be when
she's ready, not when *you* are!''

''Are you two at it again?'' Rolling her eyes,
Jenny Blackwell moved past them with the re-
quested papers in her hand.

''Hold on, Jenny.'' Keely brushed by Luke without another word. ''It's clearly too soon to push
her on this.''

''Luke—''

''Made you do it,'' Keely finished with irrita-
tion.

''Well...'' The nurse sent Luke an apologetic
look.

''Give me a minute to talk to her.'' With a pat
to Jenny's arm—ignoring Luke—Keely walked
into the examining room and approached Phyllis
Long, now huddled in a chair trying clumsily to
put on her clothes. ''Here, let me help you with
that...Phyllis, isn't it?''

"I'm okay," Phyllis mumbled, trying without success to get her arm into the long sleeve of a flannel shirt.

"I'm Dr. Hamilton," Keely said, guiding the woman's bruised hand into the sleeve. Two swollen fingers, she noted, defensive wounds no doubt incurred while trying to fend off her assailant. "Seems you're pretty banged up from that car accident."

"Uh-huh."

"Tell you what..." Keely bent and guided a bare foot into one of the woman's worn tennies. "We really need to take an X ray of those ribs and you need some sutures. What if I can persuade your husband to wait until that's done? Think you might go for that?"

"Well, I guess I could..." Phyllis wiped damp eyes with a tissue. "But I don't know how you're gonna talk him into it. He's already upset with me 'cause he had to bring me here."

Keely touched her uninjured arm gently. "You just leave that to me to worry about, okay?"

"Even if my ribs are, you know, cracked or something, I don't know what can be done about it." Sounding worried, she added, "I can't stay here. I need to get back."

Luke, standing in the door, met Keely's eyes with a what'd-I-tell-you look.

"I understand. But for starters, how about letting us give you something to ease the pain?"

She considered that. "Well..."

Keely was now sitting beside the woman. The two of them looked like best friends settling in for a nice chat. In spite of himself, Luke had to admire Keely's technique. It got results.

So what was it about the senior resident that invariably irritated him? he wondered, not for the first time. Keely was not only intelligent, confident and on a fast track to medical superstardom, she was also drop-dead beautiful. He hated to admit his reaction was rooted in the fact that he couldn't separate the professional woman from his own sexual fantasies. Fortunately, she was unaware he thought about her that way.

"One more thing, Phyllis," Keely said, "there's a guy here in the hospital you might want to talk to. Now don't freak out, okay?" She squeezed the woman's shoulder reassuringly when Phyllis immediately tensed up. "He's not a cop. He's a minister. Actually, he's the hospital chaplain. His name is Dr. Barlow, Dr. Randall Barlow." Keely smiled. "He's the soul of discretion. Anything you say to Dr. Barlow is strictly confidential and he won't go running to the authorities to stir up things you don't feel able to face right now."

Keely's tone was soft and cajoling, communicating with the woman in a manner that invited trust. As Luke watched, fascinated, Phyllis Long's demeanor changed. She visibly relaxed. If there'd been a course in touchy-feely stuff at med school, he'd missed it. Or maybe it was a woman thing. Either way, it was beyond him.

Still sitting, Keely touched a bruised hand. "Okay. You'll wait right here while I talk to your husband, won't you?"

"I guess so."

Over her head, Keely looked at Jenny. "Jenny Blackwell's your nurse. She'll stay with you while I check around to find Dr. Barlow."

"Okay."

"Meanwhile Dr. Jamison will put those sutures in for you."

"I don't want to sign those papers."

"No papers," Keely promised. "Just a conversation with Dr. Barlow."

Keely rose, the warmth in her eyes cooling abruptly as she met Luke's gaze. "Dr. Jamison, we'll have a word later."

KEELY WAS INVITED IN after a brief knock on Randall Barlow's door. The man behind the desk rose courteously, smiling in genuine welcome. "Keely, are you still here? Didn't I see you coming in this morning at seven?"

She laughed. "Peter Winstead has a flu bug, so I'm pulling a double. What's your excuse?"

"Dr. Winstead isn't the only staff member down with the flu. One of the chaplains was stricken, too." Still smiling, Randall gestured to a chair. "But sit down, sit down. I'll bet you haven't been able to grab a bite of dinner. How about a bit of yogurt? I keep some in my little fridge. Or I have fruit, if you prefer that? Apple, pear or banana. There's string cheese, too." He was shaking his head. "Whoever thought of string cheese is one clever fellow. Finger food for all ages."

"A man, was it?" Keely arched an eyebrow and sat.

"Was that a sexist assumption?" Randall asked with a rueful grin.

"Just maybe." Her smile forgave him. "But whoever, it was probably somebody with a life as busy as ours. And no, thanks, I'll pass on the snack. I'm still hoping for a real meal before the evening's completely shot."

"With a nice young man, I hope."

"I don't think that description fits Oscar very well. He's definitely not young."

"Oscar?" Randall said, looking intrigued.

"My dog. But he is nice and he's male."

Randall grinned again. "I guess I asked for that."

Keely sobered and got to the point. "Dr. Barlow, there's a battered woman in E.R. who could use your help. She's afraid of her husband and with good reason. He's currently in the waiting room causing a disturbance, but—''

Instantly Randall Barlow was on his feet, his expression stern.

''It's okay,'' Keely said, waving him back behind his desk. ''Security's handling it. The main thing is to try to get the woman some help. She's scared to death, but she's willing to talk to a minister. I thought you might be able to give her some information, maybe convince her that she has some options. She doesn't have to live her life in constant fear of what he might do next. She probably won't do anything now, but she needs to be given some information about what to do and where to call when she's ready.'' Keely leaned back. ''Maybe you're the person to give her that.''

''Sounds to me as if you could advise her as well as I, Keely. Your take on the situation and the way to handle it could have come from a handbook on abusive relationships.''

''My mother runs a halfway house for wayward teens.''

He seemed surprised. ''Really? Which one is it? Maybe I know her. I'm pretty familiar with the programs in Atlanta.''

''It's in New Orleans.''

''New Orleans?'' His face showed more pleasure. ''Your mother lives in New Orleans?''

''Yes, but—''

"I never knew that! I'm aware that you went to med school at Tulane, but I didn't know that New Orleans was your home. I grew up on Versailles, off Claiborne. Which is your neighborhood?"

Why had she strayed into a personal conversation with Randall Barlow? Keely wondered. Of all the people in the hospital, Dr. Barlow was the one person she shouldn't get chummy with. He definitely knew her mother, but she wasn't going to refresh his memory.

"I was born in Memphis," she said carefully, "not New Orleans."

"Oh." Randall studied his hands for a moment as if recalling bygone days. "Well, I haven't been to New Orleans in a while myself. To tell the truth, some of my memories aren't too pleasant. But about your patient—"

"Phyllis Long. And she's Luke Jamison's patient." Keely's tone hardened. "He took one look at her injuries and started to pressure her into taking legal action against her husband. He was completely blind to her fear. If Jenny Blackwell hadn't alerted me, Phyllis would have scurried out the back door right into the arms of the brutal creep who brought her there in the first place. He has about as much sensitivity as a tree, Dr. Barlow!"

"The creep or Luke?" Randall asked gently. ·

"Luke, of course!" She sighed. "I've told him a dozen times, he needs to *listen* to the patient more. Be open to a patient's emotional state. Don't just treat the injury, look a little deeper. But it's like talking to a…to a—''

"Tree?"

She paused, then gave an embarrassed laugh. "Listen to me, will you? I'm sorry, Doctor. That was very unprofessional. Forget everything I said.''

"Especially since we're talking about my nephew," Randall said, eyes twinkling.

Keely stared. "Your nephew?" she said weakly. "Luke Jamison is your nephew?"

"I'm afraid so." Randall rose and came around his desk, slipping a hand beneath Keely's elbow to help her to her feet. "Not a blood relative, but I'm fond of him. He's Laura's sister's oldest son. But don't worry, you're not saying anything Laura and his mother, JoEllen, haven't said many times since he left the military to begin med school.''

"I'm so embarrassed."

"Why, if you were being honest?"

"Please…''

Leaning against his desk, he asked, "Have you thought it might be…difficult for Luke to be in a subordinate position to a woman? After all, as a former Army officer, he's used to a position of command.''

"Well, he'll just have to get over it," she

snapped. "I'm the senior resident. When I leave, he can take over."

"And to add to that, you're younger, you're very smart, and you're very lovely." He was shaking his head, but his eyes were bright with amusement. "I almost feel sorry for him."

"That's another very sexist observation, Dr. Barlow," Keely said, holding back a smile. She felt a tiny thrill at his words. It was nice to know Randall Barlow thought highly of her. Maybe someday she would find the courage to tell him her secret. Or maybe not.

The chaplain ushered her in front of him and out into the hospital corridor. "I'll speak to him."

"Good luck," she said.

He chuckled at the skepticism on her face. "But for now, take me to the battered patient and introduce me. If you think I can help, I'll be happy to talk to her."

"Great." Keely headed for the elevators. "She should still be in the X-ray department, so you can talk there without the distraction of her husband. If you can persuade her that there are places where she'll be safe from him, that'll give her a glimmer of hope. For the next time."

"I'll do my best."

"I know you will." She stepped into the elevator and turned to smile at him. His eyes, a similar shade to the golden brown of her own, were warm and kind. "And thanks."

THE GLOW OF HAVING done a good deed dissolved abruptly when Keely returned to the E.R. Billy Long was still waiting for his wife. He was standing sullenly between two hospital security guards, both of whom were braced in readiness as she approached him. Before she reached him, he was moving toward her, flanked by the guards.

"Mr. Long, I'm Dr. Hamilton. I just left your wife in X-ray. I understand you're concerned about her."

"What the hell's goin' on? She just needed a coupla stitches!"

"Her injuries were more serious than that. She—"

"I want her outta here!" He pointed with a finger to the door. "And I mean *now!*" He took a step closer, ignoring the two guards. "You people got no right to keep her here when I say she should come home."

"We aren't keeping her, Mr. Long. She's having her chest X-rayed. A fractured rib can be dangerous. You wouldn't want her to suffer a punctured lung, would you?"

He looked disgusted. "Nothin' like that's gonna happen. She just had a little fender bender. If it wasn't for bustin' her chin, I wouldn't have brought her here.'' He gave a crafty smile. "She didn't want no scars messin' up her pretty face."

Keely struggled to maintain her composure. Losing her temper might mean trouble for Phyllis. Luke suddenly appeared from behind her.

"Maybe you should bear that in mind the next time you feel like hitting her, Mr. Long," he said, grim-faced.

"Hittin' her!" he roared. "Did she tell you that?"

"No, she's too frightened to tell the truth, and that's what you're counting on, isn't it?"

"I don't know what the hell you're talkin' about!"

"You can theaten desperate people only so long before they rebel, Mr. Long. Your wife has been bullied and beaten shamelessly, but don't count on her silence protecting you forever."

His small eyes narrowed with suspicion. "What kind of ideas you been puttin' in her head?"

"What makes you think we needed to plant any ideas in her head?" Luke replied. "Sooner or later she'll be desperate enough to seek help. If you're smart, you'll be out of her life before she reaches that point."

Long's hands were at his sides, opening and closing in fury. "You both had better stay out of my private business! I brought my woman here to get patched up, not to get no lectures on how to get divorced.''

Keely put a cautioning hand on Luke's arm. ''Dr. Jamison wasn't suggesting divorce, Mr. Long. He is simply concerned—''

Long thrust his head forward, threatening her with the sheer force of his rage. ''If she gets any ideas after talkin' to you, then you better look out after it's over. I'll come after you, doctor or no doctor...and that's a promise!''

Luke disregarded Keely's warning look. ''That sounds suspiciously like a threat.''

''Threat, hell! Didn't you hear me? It's a promise.''

Moving in front of Keely, Luke said, ''I'm giving you a chance to leave peacefully, Long. Otherwise, it won't be hospital security you have to deal with, but the law. Your wife may be cowed by your fists, but I don't think the police will be. And spending the night in the drunk tank won't be any picnic, either.''

''I *ain't* drunk!''

''If that's true, it's even more reason to separate you from your wife.''

''She's comin' home with me! You got no right to butt in on my private life! I don't care who you are.''

Luke signaled the security guards with a look.

"Escort this man outside and see that he waits off the premises until his wife is released."

"Yes, sir!"

Before Long could react, the guards grabbed his arms and hustled him toward the exit. He fought, cursing and struggling to free himself. Even after the doors closed behind him, his voice could be heard echoing in the night, mixing eerily with the the ding-a-linging bell of a startled Salvation Army Santa standing outside.

Keely turned to Luke. "Dr. Jamison, may I see you in the lounge?"

Luke held her gaze for a moment, then nodded curtly. "Certainly, Dr. Hamilton."

INSIDE THE LOUNGE, Keely went to the small table holding a collection of medical reading material and turned to face Luke. "What the hell did you think you were doing back there?" she demanded.

"Getting rid of a potentially dangerous piece of scum," he answered calmly.

"Don't you know what you did, Luke?" She crossed her arms. "Billy Long is dangerous and he is scum, but Phyllis is still married to him and when she leaves the hospital tonight, she's going to have to go home and face him."

"She doesn't have to face him. She can go to any of a half-dozen shelters in Atlanta."

"You just don't get it, do you? She's not ready

to ask for help. And even if you manage to persuade her to stay overnight in the hospital, she'll
go back to Billy in the morning, and he'll still be
smoldering over his humiliation in the waiting
room. Phyllis will be the one to be punished for
it.''

"Did you want me to just stand there and let
him threaten you, Keely? This is a guy who gets
off on bullying people, especially women.''

"His threats are meaningless to me! Can't you
see that? It's his wife who gets the mean end of
his fists.''

"I didn't think he was going to hit you in the
E.R. But what's to prevent him finding out where
you live and attacking you in a vulnerable moment? For a man like Long, a woman alone is easy
prey.'' He threw her own words back at her.
"Can't *you* see that?''

She dismissed his comment with a wave of her
hand. "I've had threats from bullies like him before. He's not going to attack me. His belligerence
was more pathetic than frightening.''

He was shaking his head. "I know you believe
what you're saying, but you can't assume that. I
tell you, it's dangerous to challenge a man like
Billy Long. He knows you're not afraid of him
while you're surrounded by guards in the hospital,
but if you're alone in a dark parking lot, take it

from me, you'll be scared then. And he'd take pleasure in your fear.''

"Look, I know you mean well, but I want you to know that I won't tolerate the kind of interference you showed today. For one thing, it undermines my effectiveness when you step in while I'm dealing with a difficult patient or family member. And for another, it shows a lack of respect on your part for my authority.'' She put up a hand to stop him before he could argue. "And I shouldn't have to remind you, a former military officer, of the importance of respect and order in any organization.''

Luke was silent a beat too long. "Yes, ma'am.''

"One more thing,'' she said, ignoring the glint of humor in his eye. "I've mentioned this before. You need to listen to your patients, Luke. Be sensitive to them as people, not simply as case studies to be diagnosed, treated and dismissed. If you'd stopped a moment and really *heard* what Phyllis was saying, you'd have known she wasn't receptive to outside help. Yet.''

Luke was clearly unconvinced. "Well, maybe she'll survive until she gets receptive. Then again, maybe she won't. Personally, I was unwilling to take that chance.''

Keely held his gaze, determined not to give an inch. After feeling she'd made her point, she turned on her heel and left the room.

SHE NEARLY COLLIDED with Randall Barlow as she rounded the corner heading back to the E.R.

"Oh, Dr. Barlow…" She knew she looked flustered, but thankfully the chaplain couldn't know why. "Did you have any success with Phyllis Long?"

He was shaking his head. "I'm afraid you were right about her not being ready. And there is another complication." He took her arm, steering her from the middle of the corridor to allow Luke to stride past them. "Hello, Luke."

"Randall," he greeted his uncle, but he still seemed far from happy.

"How's it going, son?"

Luke flashed a look at Keely. "Great, just great."

"Is that so?" After an amused wink at Keely, Randall said, "We'll expect you for dinner Thursday night, right? Laura's been counting on it."

Another brief glance at Keely. "As long as my schedule isn't screwed up, sure. I'll be there."

"I don't do the scheduling," Keely snapped.

"Laura will be happy to hear that." Still amused, Randall watched his nephew hurry off, white coat flapping at his thighs. As hospital tradition dictated, only senior residents wore long lab coats. Keely shoved her hands deep into her pockets and put Luke Jamison out of her mind.

"What kind of complication, Dr. Barlow?"

"Hmm?" Randall looked at her, trying to pick up the thread of the conversation. "Oh, Phyllis Long. Yes." He fell into step with Keely as they headed for the elevators. "She has a little boy, did she mention that to you?"

"No." Keely sighed with dismay. A child in that household was definitely a complication.

"He's four years old and she's terrified for the boy, but she's so intimidated by Billy that she's virtually paralyzed. It occurred to me that we might notify Social Services to look in on them before he hurts the child. Phyllis assured me that so far Billy has confined his attacks to her alone, but I wouldn't want to bet on how long his restraint will last."

"She never said a word. I'll check with the hospital administrator's office. They know the procedure to make a formal request." Keely rubbed an achy spot between her eyes. "I shudder to think of Billy Long in a fatherly role to a young child."

"Yes, it's hard to picture, isn't it?"

After a moment, Keely murmured, "Phyllis is really in a pickle."

"She is, indeed." At the elevators, Randall punched the up button. "I've seen too many women who waited too late to call for help. I hope she isn't one of them."

Stepping into the elevator with him, Keely stared worriedly at the controls. "If my mother were here, she'd think of some way to reach her. She really seems to understand the mind-set of women trapped in these relationships. Kids, too. The house used to overflow with kids who, for all practical purposes, had just been thrown away by their parents. I never knew from one day to the next who would be at the breakfast table." Her face went soft with remembrance. "Once I got up and found she'd brought home a family of seven brothers and sisters! And already we were bulging at the seams. Daniel and I got busy helping her find someplace besides our shelter to put them up."

"Daniel?"

"My stepfather. The man's a saint! He—"

Randall was smiling. "Yes, he...what?"

Keely shook her head, holding on to both ends of her stethoscope. "Sorry, when I start to babble like that, I don't seem to know when to shut up."

"Why should you? What's nicer than recalling the good times in your childhood? And it sounds as if you have very loving parents. Not many people are willing to share their lives with displaced children to the extent you've just described. You must be very proud."

"I am. My mother's wonderful. Daniel, too."

"Too bad we can't find somebody like your mom and Daniel here in Atlanta to rescue Phyllis Long."

"And her little boy."

"Yes," Randall said. The elevator stopped and as he stepped out, he turned back and added, "Before it's too late."

Keely was left alone to wonder why she'd revealed so much about herself. Not that it really mattered. Randall Barlow would never make the connection.

CHAPTER TWO

KEELY AWAKENED SUDDENLY, looking around in dazed confusion. Lord, she'd fallen asleep on the couch with the television blaring and a cup of tea balanced on her chest. It was a wonder she hadn't soaked her shirt, but luckily what little tea was left in the cup hadn't spilled. Reaching for the remote, she clicked off Jimmy Stewart in a touching moment. *It's a Wonderful Life* was one of her favorite Christmas treats, but she'd have to wait until tomorrow night to finish it. She'd put in a long day at the hospital. For some reason, the closer Christmas came, the more people seemed bent on killing themselves.

Oscar, who'd fallen asleep on the couch with her, was up and looking alert. "What is it, boy?"

He woofed just as the doorbell rang. And that's when she realized what had awakened her. Someone was at her door.

On her way to answer it, she recalled Luke's warning the other day about a lone woman's vulnerability at night. She hoped her defiance wouldn't come back to haunt her. She was defi-

nitely alone and, even though Oscar looked as if
he could hold off an attacker, the chocolate Lab
was a pussycat at heart.

She was wary as she reached the door and
peered cautiously through the peephole while at
her feet Oscar whined. Whoever it was, Oscar obviously didn't feel any imminent threat. A woman
stood hunched against blowing snow and icy wind,
turned slightly away from the tiny eye. She was
bundled into a heavy coat, the collar upturned. A
scarf covered the lower half of her face. Keely
made a startled sound of recognition.

Phyllis Long. Keely quickly turned the dead bolt
and opened the door.

"Do you remember me, Dr. Hamilton?"

"Of course, Phyllis. Come inside. It's freezing
out there." Briskly rubbing her arms and trying to
restrain Oscar at the same time, Keely waited while
Phyllis stepped inside. With her was a small boy
in a fuzzy hooded jacket. Backed against his
mother's legs, he surveyed her solemnly through
wide brown eyes.

"This is Matthew," Phyllis said, her hand resting protectively on his shoulder. "He's four."

Smiling, Keely bent to Matthew's own level.
"Hi, Matthew. I'm Keely." Beside her, Oscar
wagged his tail wildly. "And this is Oscar."

The dog woofed, making Matthew blink.

"He likes you."

He stared at the dog mutely before wiping at his tiny, red nose with a blue mitten. His mother nudged him. "Say hi to the doctor, Matty."

"Hi." His greeting was soft, almost soundless. If possible, he pressed even closer to his mother's legs.

Keely raised her eyes to Phyllis. "It's a bad night to be out, Phyllis."

"I didn't have much choice. Billy's on a rampage again."

Now Keely could see her ravaged face. She'd spoken carefully, a necessity since her jaw was bruised and swollen. One eye was purple and closing. "You need to go to the E.R. That eye needs attention and your jaw might be broken."

"I haven't got time for that, Dr. Hamilton. I'm here to ask a favor of you."

"Just call me Keely."

"Well, Dr. Keely, then."

Hoping some familiarity between them would help the woman begin to trust her, Keely pushed on. "You have to get treatment for yourself. You have Matthew to think about. What happened, for God's sake?"

"Like I said, Billy's on a rampage. But me and Matthew have left, so I don't care about Billy anymore. The problem is, he's going to be looking for us. Actually, he'll be looking for me, not Matthew."

Keely interrupted her with a bright smile. "Matthew, let's take off your coat, sweetie, and we'll go into the kitchen and find something to warm you up. Do you like hot chocolate? I can pop some milk into the microwave and we'll have some in a jiffy."

The boy looked up at his mother.

"I'm not going to sneak off, Matthew," she reassured him in an unsteady voice. "It's okay for right now. We'll just get your coat off the way Dr. Keely says and you know you love hot chocolate. 'Specially on a night like this."

"Dog."

His mother frowned. "What?"

"Oscar," Keely said, blessing the animal, who was nudging closer to the child. When he licked Matthew's face, the little boy almost smiled. Oscar was friendly, but he usually took a moment to size up a stranger. Not so with Matthew. Oscar was happy, his large tongue lolling, tail wagging ecstatically. One look and apparently Oscar was in love.

Matthew pulled off a mitten and stroked the dog's head, then he was forced to fight off another attempt to lick his small face.

"Looks as if you've found a friend, Matthew," Keely said, smiling.

The boy looked at her solemnly. "Does Oscar like hot chocolate?"

"No, but if you want some, we'll squirt whipped cream on top of it and he likes that!"

"He's a dog and he likes whipped cream?" A tiny nose wrinkled.

"Only on top of his Milk-Bones."

"Oh."

A few minutes later, Matthew was settled at Keely's small bar with a mug of chocolate topped with a squirt of artificial cream. Oscar was beside him, licking cream from his chops while gazing adoringly at the boy. Over their heads, Keely met Phyllis's eyes and they moved into the breakfast nook, still within sight of Matthew but out of earshot.

Without gloves, Keely could see the tremor in Phyllis's hands, but the woman quickly locked them together on the table in front of her. "I tried to get in touch with Dr. Barlow," she explained, looking apologetic. "He gave me his card when I was at the hospital and said I could call him in case I needed help. But he wasn't home tonight. I sure couldn't wait around my house, you can see that." A hand went to her face. "Billy..."

Keely nodded grimly. "Billy's on a rampage."

"Uh-huh."

"What's your plan, Phyllis? Do you want me to drive you to a shelter? There are a couple of really good—"

"No, that wouldn't work, Dr. Keely. It really

wouldn't. Billy'd find me no matter where I went, you can bank on that. No, I've got to leave here. I mean really leave. Take a few clothes and some money I've managed to scrape together and just start driving.'' She looked directly into Keely's eyes. ''The problem is, I can't take Matthew.''

Keely had expected something like that, but she was shocked anyway. ''You're not thinking straight, Phillis. You can't abandon your son!''

Phyllis's eyes filled. ''He's going to kill me. If Matthew's with me, he'll kill him, too. I just can't take that chance.''

Keely was shaking her head. ''No. We'll call a shelter, there's a good one—New Beginnings. It's not far from here, actually. The general public is unaware of the location, but I can get the address from a contact in Health and Human Services.''

Phyllis sighed. ''He'd find me before nightfall.''

''Then you can go to my mother in New Orleans. She's administrator of a shelter there called Sojourn. She'll take you and Matthew in. You'll be safe there, I promise!''

''I won't!'' Phyllis's voice was sharp. At the bar, Matthew looked up, his brown eyes concerned. The dog was now pushing his head onto the little boy's lap, looking for attention. ''It's okay, baby,'' Phyllis said softly, somehow managing a smile. ''Mommy's okay.''

She returned her gaze to Keely and lowered her

voice. "I won't be safe anywhere, you've got to believe me. Billy will turn over every stone. He'll lie and cheat and move mountains and he'll find me. I don't doubt that a minute. He's obsessed, Dr. Keely. He's smart, too, but...unbalanced. He's not a normal person and he plays by his rules, not the rules of ordinary people. To his mind, I belong to him and so does Matthew. Even though he's not Matthew's father!" she added bitterly.

"You're more vulnerable trying to escape on your own, Phyllis," Keely cried, running out of arguments. Echoing Luke Jamison's warning, she said, "Think of this—if Billy does find you, you'll be at his mercy, defenseless."

"No, I won't. I have a gun."

Keely blinked.

"And I'll use it if I have to."

Keely was again shaking her head. "This is crazy. You've got to let me call for help. My—I mean, Dr. Barlow and his wife will be home soon, I'm sure. Let me call him. He'll know what to do."

"He won't be able to talk me out of this, Dr. Keely. I didn't call him to ask for that kind of help. I needed something else, something more important." She put her fingers over her lips to stop them from trembling. "I need a favor and I just don't know of anybody else to ask." There was despair in her voice.

"What kind of favor?" But Keely knew. She held her breath.

"You have to take Matthew."

Keely closed her eyes. "Oh, Phyllis. No."

"You're refusing?" The woman looked ready to come apart. The eye damaged by Billy was now completely closed. She was pathetic and beaten, utterly bereft.

"No, of course I'm not refusing. I'm trying to say I don't want you to do this. You don't have to do this. No mother should be pushed to even consider such a thing. You love Matthew. You can't—"

"I do love him, more than life itself. And it's because I love him so much that I'm asking you to take him, just until you can reach Dr. Barlow and beg him and his wife to keep Matthew for me until I feel it's safe to come back for him."

"You said Billy would never give up searching for you."

"Then I'll just have to take care of that…somehow."

"WHEN'S MY MOMMY coming back?"

Keely plumped a cushion on the couch and reached for a soft, warm throw decorated in a Christmas motif. Then she sat down and patted the space beside her. Obediently Matthew crawled up next to her and so did Oscar. Keely tucked the throw around the little boy and snuggled him close. His face was streaked with tears and he was still hiccuping from crying so hard when Phyllis had finally left. Keely was no stranger to traumatized children. Since her early teens, she'd been rescuing at-risk kids from the streets of New Orleans with her mother. But Keely had never witnessed a scene as wrenching as when Phyllis said goodbye to Matthew a few minutes ago. The woman truly might never see her son again, which made the parting so much more painful. But how to prepare a four-year-old for such a devastating possibility?

"Your mommy has to take a trip, Matthew. An important trip. She told you that, remember? She isn't sure exactly when she'll be back, but it will be just as quick as she can."

Matthew swiped at his nose. "I d-don't want to stay with Billy while sh-she's away."

"I know that. And you won't have to. You won't even see Billy while she's away." Fighting her own tears, Keely put an arm around the boy's small shoulders. "Your mommy said you could stay with me until her business was all done."

After a moment, he nodded. And then he asked, "Where will I sleep?"

"Right down the hall. I have a nice room with a bed that has a soft, fuzzy blanket and lots of pillows."

"Can Oscar sleep with me?"

Keely looked at the dog, who met her gaze hopefully. "What d'ya say, Oz?"

"You call him Oz?" Matthew asked.

"It's short for Oscar, you know? Like Matty's short for Matthew."

"Only my mommy calls me Matty," he told her.

"I'll remember that."

"So can Oz sleep with me?"

"You bet."

The boy nodded. "Then I guess I'll be okay here for a while."

The doorbell rang.

With a sharp bark, Oscar jumped from the couch and stood protectively between Matthew and the front door. Matthew scrambled down and, with a look of panic, appeared to search for a place to hide.

"It's okay, Matthew," Keely said, putting both hands on his shoulders and forcing him to look at her. "We're not going to open the door to anybody we don't know."

"We know Billy!" the boy cried. "If it's him, don't open it anyway!"

"If it's Billy, I won't open it," Keely assured him. "You can wait in the bedroom with Oscar if you want to."

"Okay." The boy dashed off with Oscar at his heels. As she headed for the foyer, she heard him slam the bedroom door, hard. Matthew's fear was contagious. Her own heart was racing. Even though the chances were slim, what if it was Billy? What if he'd somehow figured out what Phyllis had planned?

At the door, she checked the peephole and, for a second, stared in disbelief at Luke Jamison's face. Releasing a sigh, she opened the door.

"What are you doing here?"

"Can I come in?" He was in a leather bomber jacket and worn jeans. On his feet were the battered high-top Rockports he worked in and on his head was a baseball cap with an Atlanta Falcons logo. He looked rumpled and tired, but all male. He filled up her tiny foyer, which he was surveying with open curiosity.

"It's nearly midnight."

"I know, but I thought I saw Phyllis Long leaving the complex as I was turning in."

The complex was located conveniently near the hospital. Several of Keely's co-workers leased apartments there, including Luke. But he'd never visited her, nor had she ever been inside his place. She stepped back now to let him in. "You're not going to believe this, but Phyllis has finally decided to leave Billy."

"Well, great." Closing the door, Luke pulled off his cap and used it to brush snow from his jacket and jeans. He wore no gloves, she noted. In fact, he seemed particularly underdressed for cold, wet weather, but it didn't seem to faze him. "Did she come here to tell you that?" he asked.

"Not exactly." Just then, the door of her guest bedroom squeaked and Oscar bounded out, heading directly for Luke. Stopping short, he bristled suspiciously. The dog wasn't naturally hostile to strangers. Keely suspected he was sensitive to Matthew's fear and was making sure this intruder was no threat to his young charge.

She put a hand on the dog's head. "It's okay, Oz." To Luke, she explained, "Oz and I have a guest."

"Ah, jeez, I've interrupted something." Looking embarrassed, Luke put the baseball cap back on his head and turned to leave.

Keely stopped him. "No, wait. It's not what you think." She removed her hand from his arm. "Phyllis wasn't alone when she came by." Just then, Matthew emerged shyly from the bedroom. "This is her son." Keely reached for the boy and pulled him in front of her, resting both hands on his shoulders, much as his mother had done an hour ago. "Matthew, this is Dr. Luke Jamison."

LUKE HAD MADE UP HIS MIND years before that he didn't want kids of his own. His father, an Army officer, had been brutal and unloving, demanding from Luke and his younger brother standards of achievement that had been virtually impossible to meet. Luke's brother had given up trying in his early teens, expressing his rebellion with drugs and alcohol, then he'd simply walked away. He hadn't even shown up for the old man's funeral. It had been four years since Luke had heard from Michael.

Luke's decision to have a career in the Army after graduating from college was an attempt to please his father. That was hindsight. He hadn't known it then. He'd only gained perspective on everything after a tragedy in the field had left blood on his hands. That chunk of his life explained his lateness in entering medical school. Sometimes he felt twenty years older than the other residents.

Kids made Luke nervous. His own childhood was marked by moments of terror, unhappiness and pain with precious little of the carefree joy most kids took for granted. Even before the disastrous experience in Bosnia—which precipitated his decision to end his military career—he was convinced he was ill equipped to be a father. He believed the conventional wisdom that kids from abusive childhoods grew up to repeat the sins of their fathers. For him, it wouldn't happen. He didn't intend to ever become a father.

"H'lo, mister." The big-eyed kid was staring up at him. Looked as if he'd been crying, too.

"Hello...Matthew, you say?"

"Yeah. Sometimes my mom calls me Matty, but I don't want you to. It sounds like a baby name, and I ain't no baby."

Luke glanced from the boy to Keely and back again. "How old are you then? Eight, ten?"

Matthew almost smiled. "No! You're way off. I'm four." He stuck up four fingers. "See? But I'll be five soon. How old are you?"

"Old enough," Luke said.

"Old enough for what?"

Okay, the kid was going to take everything he said literally. "I'm old enough to be awake at midnight. But I don't think you are."

"That's exactly what I was just about to say," Keely said, with a hand on the boy's neck. "Matthew, Oscar needs his rest if he's going to be a good watchdog for us. Come on, let's get into that great T-shirt your mommy left for you to sleep in and we'll put ol' Oz right on the bed at your feet. He'll keep you warm and he'll protect you. How does that sound?"

"He won't let Billy into my room, will he?"

"Absolutely not."

"Well, okay." Matthew slipped his hand into hers.

"Tell Dr. Jamison good-night."

With his hand securely in Keely's, Matthew turned to look back at Luke. "G'night, mister."

"I DON'T KNOW WHY he calls you mister."

"He's establishing his territory," Luke said, taking a seat in the breakfast room. Keely had offered him a cup of coffee after getting the boy settled for the night. He could be pushing the bounds of polite behavior by staying when he knew she'd put in a killer of a day—as he had. But he wanted to hear how in hell she'd been saddled with Phyllis Long's kid.

"All that kid's male instincts are in working order," Luke said. "He's uprooted from everything that's familiar and essentially his, including his mother. You're a surrogate, at least for a while. Added to that, there is no other male on the premises, at least, none that he's seen. Therefore, he's the king of the cave. And I'm trespassing."

"That's ridiculous!" Keely laughed as she set a mug filled with coffee in front of him. "He's just a little boy."

Luke shrugged, declining to argue. Picking up the mug, he surveyed her over the rim. "So, what's the story, Keely? Where is Phyllis? How long will she be gone?"

"The story in a nutshell is that 'Billy's on a rampage.'" Keely sat down, cradling her warm mug in both hands. "Those are Phyllis's words, not mine. As to where she is and how long she'll be gone, your guess is as good as mine."

"She just left her kid and skipped out?"

"It wasn't like that." Keely stared into her coffee. "If you could have heard her, you wouldn't say that. When I watched her telling her little boy goodbye…" She shook her head. "It was terrible. It was enough to break your heart."

"She can't just leave him here. How does she expect you to care for him? You don't exactly sit around all day with nothing to do. You've got a demanding job, and she knows that."

"Matthew's only going to be here for one night. Phyllis wants Randall Barlow to keep him until she comes back for him."

Luke looked unconvinced. "I don't know about that. True, Randall's a likely person to turn to, but I wouldn't count on him if I were you."

"Why not?" She was frowning. "He's a minister. If a woman in jeopardy can't rely on a man of the cloth, who's left?"

"Worst-case scenario?" Luke stood up and reached for his jacket. "There's always Health and Human Services."

Keely was already on her feet. "Matthew's not going to HHS to be shunted off to some foster family…to people he doesn't know and who don't know a thing about him."

"You didn't know him until a few hours ago, Keely."

"His mother left him in my care," she said, her mouth set stubbornly. "I'm to take him to Randall

Barlow where he's to stay until Phyllis comes to get him!''

He stared at her. ''Think about it! You expect my aunt and uncle to take in a four-year-old child? Minister or not, that's a big responsibility. I'm telling you, don't count on it. They lost their daughter in a car accident two years ago, and they're not over it yet, not by a long shot. At least, Laura isn't. They'll feel sorry for a kid who's been abandoned by his mother, but bringing him home to live with them, even temporarily, isn't in the cards. Take it from me.''

''She didn't abandon him! Didn't you yourself say if she stayed, someday Billy might kill her? Well, that moment arrived. She left tonight in fear of her life and that of her son. Her face was so battered and swollen she could hardly see out of one eye. The woman was desperate. She had no choice.'' Keely paused, looking grim. ''She has a gun, Luke.''

Luke shrugged into his jacket. ''Then the next time you hear about her, it'll probably be through the Coroner's Office.''

''That's a terrible thing to say!''

''It's the truth. She's fleeing from a maniac and she thinks she can protect herself because she has a weapon.'' He grabbed his keys and his baseball cap. ''Is she trained to use it?''

''I don't know.''

He grunted, unsurprised.

"I cautioned her about it," Keely said, sounding uncertain. "But she was desperate. All of which is beside the point where Matthew's concerned. She asked me to take him to Randall Barlow and that's what I'm going to do."

"And what if Randall does what I think he will? What if he says taking on the care of a four-year-old boy is not something he chooses to do?"

Her chin lifted. "That's a problem I'll handle when it happens." She waited until he got to the door and opened it. Icy wind whipped at the landscaping around her stoop, chilling her instantly. On the eaves, icicles were already forming. She shivered, thinking of Phyllis fleeing Billy's wrath this cold, dark night. "But whatever happens, Matthew isn't going to be a throwaway child. If need be, I'll take him."

CHAPTER THREE

KEELY HADN'T ASKED LUKE to go with her to the Barlows', but for some reason it had been the first thought to hit him when he rolled out of bed next morning at eight, rather than at noon, which was his usual habit after working an extended shift. But if Keely was hell-bent on following through with her plan, he was going along to keep her from putting any unnecessary pressure on his aunt. Having a kid dropped on your doorstep wasn't like taking in a puppy. Feeding, housing and clothing Matthew was one thing, but there was an emotional commitment involved that Laura might not be up to.

Keely seemed a little surprised when she opened the door and saw him, but she agreed readily when he suggested accompanying her and Matthew to the Barlows'.

"Thanks for coming with us," she said, giving him a nervous smile after getting into the passenger seat of Luke's Explorer. She cast a quick glance at Matthew, who was in the back seat listening to a tape on her Walkman. Apparently satisfied that he was unable to hear their conversation, she fastened her seat belt. "I admit I'm a little anxious over the outcome of all this."

"With good reason," Luke said as he drove off. "What happens if nobody's home?"

"They're home. I called and Dr. Barlow said ten o'clock was convenient. He was curious about why I wanted to see him, but I thought it was better to explain in person."

"Yeah." He looked in the rearview mirror. "This isn't exactly the kind of proposition you want to put to somebody over the phone."

She gave an exasperated sound. "If you're so set on being negative about this, why are you going with us?"

She had a right to be confused, Luke thought. He'd hurried over this morning with a vague plan to try to persuade her to look for another solution that wouldn't involve his aunt and uncle. "Vague" didn't work with Keely Hamilton. Just as she dug in her heels at the hospital in support of her favorite projects, she wasn't budging from her belief that Matthew's place was with the Barlows. That was Phyllis's choice and Keely was determined to make it happen.

"I'm asking myself the same question," Luke said with a shrug. "Why am I going? I guess I'm an advocate for Laura and Randall."

"Excuse me, but it's Matthew who's the child

here," she said, crossing her arms. "If anybody needs representation, it's him. If the Barlows don't want to honor Phyllis's request, all they have to do is say no."

"As if you'd take no for an answer without an argument." He gave a snort, stopping for a traffic light. "I've seen you at the hospital defending an issue you didn't feel half as passionate about. I just don't want to see the Barlows pressured to do something they're not ready to face. Especially Laura."

"You're not going to argue against them taking Matthew, are you?"

"No. But I'm not going to push them, either."

For a minute, Keely's gaze followed a man jogging with his dog. "Tell me a little about Shelley. I know she was killed in an accident."

"Yeah. Two years ago. She was in Colorado skiing with friends during the holidays. It happened on New Year's Eve."

"I remember." And she did, vividly.

"My mother said she wondered for a while whether Laura would survive it. Shelley was a great girl—smart, pretty, outgoing. Everybody loved her."

Keely looked at him. "I know it was a drunk driver."

"Then you know he died, too. Otherwise, I

don't think anything less than life in prison would have satisfied Randall.''

''Was she a 'daddy's girl'?'' Keely studied her hands.

''I don't know about that. I've been away from Atlanta for a long time. But neither of them mentions it, ever.''

''You said she was pretty.''

After shooting her a quick glance, he signaled to turn into a gated neighborhood. ''She looked a lot like you, now that I think about it—same streaky blond hair, about your height. The eyes…well, your eyes are different. Hers were…'' he frowned ''—blue, I think. Yeah, like Laura's.''

''So we had height and hair color in common,'' Keely said, watching him punch in a security code to open the gates. ''Doesn't sound like a whole lot of similarities to me.''

''Guess not. It was just a thought.'' Luke turned to look at her, wondering where his idea that they were alike had come from. Dismissing it, he put the Explorer in gear and drove into the neighborhood. ''Shelley was only eighteen when it happened, a freshman in college. But still just a kid.''

''Is this where they live?'' Keely gazed at the graceful Victorian lines of the house as Luke pulled into a curved driveway. Horseshoe steps swept up to twin leaded-glass doors that glistened in the morning sun. Keely was reminded of the old residences in New Orleans's Garden District. Randall Barlow may have left the Crescent City, but he hadn't rejected its architectural heritage. Looking at the elaborate gingerbread that adorned the eaves and windows, she realized suddenly how long it had been since she'd been home. It would be great to see her mother.

Which made her wonder what her mother would think if she knew where Keely was at this minute and whose house she was about to enter. Shaking off that thought, she jumped from the Explorer and opened the rear door to help Matthew out of his seat belt.

"I can do it!" he told her, proving it by freeing himself and scrambling out of the car. "Who lives here?" the boy asked, as wide-eyed as Keely had been a moment before.

"A very nice man and a sweet lady. You'll like them."

"Do they know my mommy?"

"The nice man does. He met your mommy a few days ago."

"Okay." He slipped his hand into Keely's, gazing up into her face. "But I'm staying with you, okay? 'Cause that's where my mommy will look for me when she comes back!"

Keely and Luke exchanged a glance over his head as they climbed the steps, then Luke reached forward and rang the doorbell.

After a few moments, the door was opened by Randall Barlow. "Hi, Keely. And Luke!" Smiling, he shook his nephew's hand. "I wasn't expecting you. Laura will be tickled. And who's this?" He gave Matthew a friendly look.

"This is Matthew, Dr. Barlow," Keely said, aware that the boy was pressing warily against her. She was suddenly uncertain of her mission. She was carrying out Phyllis's request, wasn't she? It wasn't as if Matthew was being abandoned for the second time in less than twelve hours.

"Hello, Matthew," Randall said, smiling, although he looked puzzled as he met Keely's eyes.

"Matthew is Phyllis Long's son," she explained, hoping from the tone of her voice that he would hold his questions.

"Ahh." Randall nodded with understanding, although he was still clearly confused. Luke was no help, remaining mute as a mop. Keely threw him an exasperated look. Since he was close to the Barlows, she'd counted on him to break the ice. Why had he offered to come with her if he was just going to stand there?

Once inside, Randall ushered them through a gorgeous foyer decorated with fresh evergreen boughs and touches of Christmas everywhere. They eventually reached a family room at the rear of the house where Laura Barlow sat near a reading lamp, an open book in her hands. The room was warm and welcoming. A lavish Christmas tree stood in front of a wall of windows. A cheery fire crackled in the fireplace. Laura rose from her chair with a coolly surprised look. For a reason that Keely had never figured out, Laura Barlow acted distant, although polite, around her.

"Hello, Dr. Hamilton. And Luke, how nice to see you." She lifted her cheek to be kissed by her nephew.

"Please," Keely said, "I'm Keely. I'm sorry to intrude, but—"

"Nonsense." Ever gracious, Laura smiled at Matthew. "And you've brought a little friend."

"Matthew is staying with me for a while," Keely said, ignoring the look Luke sent her. What did he expect her to do? Jump right in and say this is Matthew and he'll soon be living here with you?

Luke finally spoke. "Do you still have some of those Christmas cookies with shapes like bells and angels, Laura? I bet Matthew would like to sample a few."

"Indeed I do," Laura Barlow said after a moment of hesitation. She put out a hand to the boy. "Come with me, Matthew, and we'll see if I can remember which pretty box I put them in."

Matthew looked at Keely. "Don't go anywhere, Keely."

"I won't, honey bun," she said firmly. "I promise."

"Now, what's this all about?" Randall Barlow said as soon as Laura and the boy were gone.

Keely drew in a deep breath. This was tougher than she'd imagined. "Phyllis Long tried to reach you last night but you and Mrs. Barlow were out."

"Please…" He stopped her with a raised hand. "Surely we've worked together long enough for you to call me Randall. And my wife is Laura."

Keely hesitated only a heartbeat. "Okay. As I was saying, Phyllis was running away. She'd been attacked by Billy again and this time she was convinced he meant to kill her. She wanted me to take Matthew in for the night, but to bring him over to you this morning. She made me promise. She wants you to keep him until she thinks it's safe to return."

Randall sat down with a resigned sigh. "Yes, well, I'm not surprised to hear this, I must say. I was concerned for her son from the first. And now it's happened." He was shaking his head and looking grave. "And of course I'll do my best to find a place for the boy. I'm in touch with some really good people who will be happy to take him in for a while. But I have to say, Keely, he seems very attached to you. Be prepared for a scene when you try to leave him."

"You don't understand." Keely moved forward on the soft couch, clasping her hands. "Phyllis asked that you personally take Matthew. She doesn't want him to go to a foster home."

He frowned. "I understand her concern, but I'm afraid it's not as simple as that." He rushed on before she could speak. "My wife would have to agree."

Sensing reluctance, Keely pushed. "It wouldn't be forever. And you know how dismal some foster care situations can be."

"I would see to it that Matthew wouldn't get trapped in anything like that," the minister replied.

Keely rose suddenly and began to pace. "But you can't be sure! Some foster parents are perfectly respectable, but to others, the care of children is simply a source of income. Worse yet, a few are abusive. Matthew's just been rescued from an abusive situation. I don't want him to escape that only to be put in another!"

She saw by the look on their faces that her speech had aroused their curiosity, but she was on a roll. "Believe me, you don't know what lurks out there for vulnerable children."

"And you do?" Randall questioned her softly.

She looked away. "I was in a lot of foster homes when I was young."

"How young?" Luke asked.

She shrugged. "What difference does it make? Take my word for it, Matthew won't be shunted off into that hell."

Randall was frowning. "You didn't live with your mother as a child? I think you said she's in New Orleans?"

"She is. And she's a wonderful person. She…she was unable to take care of me…then. She…had problems. She thought I'd be better off in foster care than with her, but I wasn't. Besides, this isn't about me." She looked at Randall pleadingly. "I just can't risk putting Matthew in a situation that could damage him more than he already has been."

"What about your father?" Again it was Luke asking.

She hesitated. "He…I never knew him."

"By choice or because he wasn't around?"

She gave a humorless laugh. "Do you honestly think I'd have stayed a ward of the state for all those years if I'd been able to go to my father? Hardly. I don't think he knew I even existed."

"A ward of the state?"

"Luke." Randall broke in. "Perhaps this is a conversation you'll want to have in private with Keely." He smiled chidingly. "If at all."

It was a moment before Luke reacted. "Oh, hell. You're right." He gave Keely an apologetic shrug. "Sorry, I was out of line."

"It's okay. But now maybe both of you understand why I'm so concerened about Matthew. I know what I'm talking about. I promised Phyllis I'd do what she asked." She looked at Randall. "She wanted you and your wife to take Matthew until she returned, Dr. Barlow."

"Randall, Keely. Randall." The minister got slowly to his feet.

"Will you take Matthew?" she asked.

"Quit pushing, Keely," Luke said, leaving his chair. "I've seen Army sergeants less tenacious than you!"

"The boy isn't going to let you abandon him so easily, Keely," Randall said, ignoring Luke. "Seems to me he's looking to you as sort of a stand-in for his mother until she returns."

"Don't use that word!" Keely cried. "I'm not abandoning him. Thrusting him into the clutches of Social Services is abandonment."

"He might see anything short of staying with you as abandonment," Randall suggested quietly.

"There are only two options here," she said stubbornly.

"It's you or me, right?" Randall replied.

"Yes."

Randall sighed. "I'm just not sure that Laura will go for it. I wish she would. In fact, I'd be delighted if she would. But—"

Keely brightened. "You'd be willing if she agreed?"

"Only because I don't see how you could possibly take on the responsibility for a four-year-old with your busy life," Randall said.

"All right!" Keely rubbed her hands together. "Do you want us to wait here while you talk to Laura?"

Smiling, Randall turned to Luke. "Is this the way she manages those hapless interns at the hospital?"

"Except for one thing," Luke said, a wicked grin on his face. "Out of respect for you, she didn't bring her bullwhip."

"I CAN'T BELIEVE you're even suggesting such a thing, Randall." Laura Barlow moved to the window of their bedroom and stood looking out. "Do you know what day this is?"

Randall lowered himself into the chair. Keely and Luke waited in the family room with the boy. He'd known as soon as he'd asked what his wife's decision would be. "No, what day is it?"

"It was on this day that Shelley made her last visit home. She was leaving for Colorado the following Monday. It was her only chance to do—" voice rising slightly, Laura touched her throat "—Christmas shopping. She and I went together."

"I had forgotten. I'm sorry," he said quietly.

"I don't forget anything. *Anything!*" She turned to him. "And now you want me to open my house to another child? It's impossible, Randall."

"I thought it might be a chance for you to perhaps…focus on other things."

Laura's eyes were bright with tears. "Focusing on other things won't bring Shelley back!"

"Nothing will bring Shelley back. She's…lost to us now. But we have to keep on going."

Her face twisted. "What you'd really like to say is that Shelley's dead, isn't it? Shelley's dead but we're alive. Well, saying it doesn't make it acceptable to me." She pressed fingers to her mouth. "Nothing can ever make it acceptable."

"Ah, Laura, Laura…" He was shaking his head. "You've got to move beyond that. You've got to let it go."

She lifted her shoulders helplessly. "How?"

A wave of weariness rolled over him. Did she think he knew the answer to that? If he did, he wouldn't wake every morning to his own pain. And it wouldn't be the last thought in his head at night.

"Maybe there's some hidden purpose here," he suggested, searching for something to turn his wife's attention from their devastating loss. "The boy needs a home and his mother has asked us to take him in. I tried to persuade her a few days ago to get help. She was battered and beaten, but she wasn't receptive then. And now she's run away, apparently fearing her husband means to kill her. I can't just ignore her request, Laura."

"Why not? There are agencies. There's Health and Human Services. There are shelters for abandoned children."

"To her mind, she hasn't abandoned her child. I think she believes she's protecting him by drawing the wrath of her husband toward her and away from the boy."

"And what if her husband finds him here? Have you thought of that?"

"We have a good security system. And the guard wouldn't allow a stranger through the gate."

"If he chose to enter by the gate," Laura said. Then she waved her hand. "This is pointless. It's not a safety issue. It's more than that and you know it. Christmas is a hard time for me. I don't want the added burden of a child when the anniversary of our daughter's death is coming up!"

"He's four years old, Laura. Don't assume he would be a reminder of hurtful things. It might be just the opposite. Give him a chance!"

Laura pulled a tissue from a box and sat on the edge of the bed. "I don't want to do this, Randall," she said firmly. "As your wife, I've had no choice all these years but to play a role that has sometimes been...difficult for me. I've smiled and made nice. I've bitten my tongue when I'd have preferred to tell somebody off. I've done charitable works. I've cooked and sewed and volunteered until I thought I would scream! But always I had to remember your position, your commitment, your holy calling."

She stood up, wiping her nose with the tissue and tossing it into a wastebasket. "Well, this is one thing I won't do, and I don't want to hear any more about it!"

CHAPTER FOUR

KEELY CAME OUT OF THE BATHROOM, leaving Matthew barely visible above a mountain of bubbles. She had purchased kiddie bubble bath at a supermarket after leaving the Barlows. Surprisingly, when she'd reached the checkout, Luke was waiting with an assortment of goodies, plastic tub toys, a coloring book and crayons. And now Matthew was busy squirting "water bullets" at animal shapes he'd stuck on the tile wall. Oscar had fled after getting a snoutful.

"Good choice," she told Luke, accepting the glass of merlot he offered as she walked into the living room. The dog, half asleep under the coffee table, opened one eye, then apparently satisfied that all was well, dozed off.

"The wine or the toys?" He pushed some of Matthew's things aside and sat down on her couch.

"Both. This is a nice merlot." With a sigh, she sank into her favorite chair. "I don't remember you checking it out at the supermarket."

"I didn't. I had it at my place. I went over and

picked it up while you were getting Matthew into the tub.''

"Good thinking." She saluted him with the glass, then settled deeper into the big chair. After a moment, she smiled. "I'm bushed! A four-year-old boy can really use up energy."

"I'll say."

"I bet he asked a thousand questions and said a million words."

Luke stretched out his long legs and crossed them at the ankles. "I thought you were used to little kids. Your mom runs a shelter, you said?"

"Not for little ones, only teens. My aunt Stephanie has three children, but I haven't really spent much time with them. I've been busy in med school and then doing my residency."

He balanced his wineglass on his belly. "You like kids." It was not a question.

"Yeah." Keely smiled, listening to Matthew talk to himself in the bathroom. Occasionally he laughed out loud. Considering his predicament and the turbulence he must have sensed in his home, it amazed Keely that he wasn't more withdrawn or more suspicious of other people, especially strangers. Instead, he seemed remarkably trusting. Phyllis Long might have been held hostage by an abusive husband, but she'd somehow managed to shield her son. Of course, only time would tell.

She got up and walked down the hall to the bathroom to be sure Matthew couldn't overhear their conversation, but he was happily occupied. She left the door ajar and went back to the living room. Settling once more in the big chair, she picked up her wineglass and asked, "What about you?"

"What about me?"

"Do you like kids?"

"I don't know any."

She laughed. "Come on. Everybody knows one or two. They're in and out of the E.R. constantly."

"Let's just say I feel more comfortable with adults."

She was intrigued now. "I didn't notice that with Matthew today. Besides, kids are funny. They seem to have some kind of built-in radar that tells them who they can trust and who they can't."

"Matthew's okay."

"You just don't want to get too close, right?" She watched him sit up, drink a little wine and glance toward the door as if thinking about escape—all signs that she was getting too personal. "Were you an only child?"

"What makes you ask?"

She smiled. "Just nosy. I like to know about people."

He shrugged. "I have a brother."

"Older? Younger?"

"Younger."

"I know your mother is Laura Barlow's sister. Randall mentioned her. JoEllen."

"You have a good memory," he said, but it didn't sound like a compliment.

"How about your father?"

"Dead."

She waited for him to volunteer something else. Amazing how curious she was about Luke. She'd learned precious little so far, but was it necessary to know his secrets? She wasn't starting a relationship with the man, just trying to find a way to help a little boy. She was thinking of getting up and starting something for dinner when Luke began to talk.

"I was an Army brat." He sat hunched over, twirling his wineglass between his palms. "Because of my father's career, we moved around a lot. You don't have much opportunity to make friends with other kids when you're always the new kid on the block. Maybe that's why I'm a little skittish."

"Matthew will soon cure you of that," she said confidently. "He's a darling."

"Yeah—well, I guess I have a missing gene or something."

She didn't believe it. He'd been too good with Matthew, too easy. Gentle and sensitive. But she knew when it was best to say nothing. She'd leave winning him over to Matthew himself.

Draining the last of the wine, he set his glass aside and lowered his voice so that she barely heard him. "So now you see why I don't exactly feel qualified to play a big role in the life of any kid."

"Not really," she said, although she'd been touched by the lonely picture he'd painted of his childhood. "But it does sound as if you know some things you'd change if you were a father."

"Fortunately, I'm not playing the role of father in Matthew's life."

"Somebody has to."

He gave her a direct look. "And are you willing to be his mother?"

"Unlike you, I haven't given up on the Barlows yet. Today was just the first shot over the bow. The battle is yet to be engaged."

He couldn't help laughing. "You sound like a general planning a military campaign."

She smiled into her wine. "I thought you'd appreciate the symbolism."

He was immediately suspicious. "Why?"

She looked at him as if he needed a brain transplant. "Because you're going to help me."

In one lithe movement, he was on his feet. "The hell you say."

She was shaking her head, but as she got up out of the chair, she spilled some of her wine. "Now look what I've done! Here, give me a hand. Take this, will you?''

But instead of taking the glass, he surprised her by bringing her forward in a rush and trapping her against him. All of him. Startled, she put one hand out, bracing it against his chest. The other still held her wineglass. She looked up and forgot whatever she was about to say.

''Careful,'' he said, a heartbeat from her mouth. ''You'll spill the rest of it.''

''I'm okay.'' But she sounded breathless and utterly unlike herself. This close, she could see his gray eyes were a crystallike mix of blue and silver, ringed in black. And he was taller than she'd realized. He held her within the circle of his arms, making her feel small and feminine. No man ever made her feel small. The feminine part, well, she'd think about that one later.

''You can let me go now,'' she said, still sounding like a stranger to her own ears. Oscar was on his feet watching them both with interest. Luke ignored him.

''What was that about a military campaign?'' He was studying her lips.

''I was just kidding.'' She could smell his aftershave, faint after a day's wear, but definitely there. She liked it.

''And were you kidding when you suggested I should help you browbeat my aunt and uncle into doing something they absolutely don't want to do?'' Now his eyes roamed over her whole face. Keely's heart was beating like a runaway train. Was he going to kiss her? Somewhere deep inside her, she tingled, waiting...

She blinked as he relaxed his hold.

''You won't have to do any browbeating,'' she told him, realizing that she was the only one thinking about a kiss. Then a devil came alive inside her. ''I'll do all the browbeating that's necessary.''

She squealed and leaped out of reach as he grabbed for her again, swearing. ''Damn it, Keely! Didn't you hear a word I said?''

She darted behind the huge chair, holding him off with her wine. ''Don't swear!'' she hissed, laughing as Oscar barked with excitement. ''Matthew might hear you.''

''He can probably swear better than me,'' Luke growled, but he put a calming hand on the dog's head.

''Yeah.'' Keely's smile faded. ''He's probably heard a lot worse than that from Billy.''

''Which brings us back to the original problem. What next?''

She drew in a deep breath. ''I wish I knew.''

Keely went to the coffee table and poured them both another glass of wine. She gave Luke his glass and they both sipped, looking at each other.

His gaze dropped to her mouth just as Matthew called out her name.

"What is it, Matthew?" she called back.

"Why is Oscar barking?"

"He's happy."

"Oh. Don't go anywhere, okay?" the little boy said.

"No way, I'm right here."

"I don't want Luke to go anywhere, either." Water splashed as he sloshed around in the tub.

Keely lifted one eyebrow, her gaze still locked with Luke's. "He's here, too."

"He has to stay with us tonight to take care of us!" Matthew stated.

Luke tossed back most of the wine. "Wouldn't it be better to just go into the bathroom to have this conversation?" he grumbled.

"We've got Oscar to take care of us," Keely reminded Matthew. "Remember?"

"Okay." More splashing. "I like Oscar."

Hearing his name, Oscar trotted off in the direction of the bathroom.

"He has a point, Keely," Luke said in a low tone. "Billy's sure to be looking for Phyllis and he's just crazy enough to threaten anybody who might have helped her run away."

"He'll have to put it together first," Keely said, taking a moment to consider Luke's words. Then she shook her head. "Nah. I bet he's checking out all their friends…if they have any…for clues as to her whereabouts. And the phone bill. And her credit cards…''

"If she has any."

"True." Keely headed for the kitchen to begin fixing something for Matthew to eat. "No, I'm not worried about Billy. My biggest concern right now is what to do about Matthew on Monday morning when I have to be at the hospital at seven.''

"Even if you knew any baby-sitters, I can't see him accepting a stranger. When you head for the door, he's going to freak out.''

"Jenny Blackwell's daughter, Chloe, is home from college for the Christmas holidays. She might be able to help. I'll ask tomorrow. But at best, that's only a temporary fix for the problem." Keely put a frozen entrée in the microwave and punched in a command before turning to look at him. "Like I said, I'm scheduled for seven o'clock Monday morning, so I have until then to figure something out. When are you going in?''

"I'm on evenings," he said, leaning against the counter. "Four to midnight. You ought to know, it was your—'' He stopped when he saw the look on her face.

"Uh-uh, no way!"

"What?" she said. "I haven't said anything yet.''

"I know that look, Keely. I'm no baby-sitter. I

don't know a goddamn thing about kids. Didn't you hear anything I said? What the hell would I do all day to entertain—''

A childish voice stopped him. "I heard you cussin', Luke."

Matthew, wet and haphazardly clutching a towel, stood looking at them. Water glistened on his arms and a trail of footprints stretched behind him all the way from the bathroom. Beside him, Oscar panted, and wagged his tail.

Keely moved quickly to his side. "You're gonna freeze, kiddo. Here, let me dry you off." She began briskly rubbing him down. "Your Skivvies are in your duffel on the couch. We need to get you dressed so you can warm up, what d'ya say?"

Coming up out of the fluffy towel, Matthew looked confused. "What's Skivvies?"

She glanced at Luke.

"Joe Boxers?" he suggested.

"I don't got none of that," Matthew stated flatly. "I just got my jammies!"

"Oh, right, that's what I meant to say." Smiling, Keely found a pair of tiny briefs and pajamas decorated with scenes from *Star Wars*. When Matthew was dressed, she sent him into the bathroom to get a hairbrush. Oscar trotted happily beside him.

"See?" she said to Luke. "Neither of us knows a whole heck of a lot about little boys, but we can muddle through. We have to."

"I don't have to do anything."

She glanced back to make sure Matthew couldn't hear before hissing, "You're in this whether you like it or not! If you hadn't wanted to get involved, you wouldn't have gone with Matthew and me to see the Barlows this morning."

"It didn't have anything to do with Matthew. I knew you'd roll over those two like a Sherman tank to get your way!"

"Because it's the right thing to do!"

He threw up his hands in exasperation. "Who appointed you judge for what's right?"

Her finger zeroed in on his chest, almost touching it. "Who appointed you to run interference for the Barlows?"

He looked away, as if gathering patience, before facing her again. "Ask yourself this, Keely. If it was the right thing for Randall and Laura to take the kid, it wouldn't be necessary to conduct a military campaign to defeat their objections, would it? They'd do it without you lifting a finger. And if baby-sitting was the right thing for me to do, I'd feel some kind of...of connection with Matthew. And I don't. Can't you see that?"

"You're just throwing up obstacles for the hell of it," Keely said with an impatient shrug. "Phyllis is counting on me."

"Fine! Go ahead then." He shrugged into his jacket. "Just don't count on me!"

"WHERE'RE WE GOIN' NOW?" Hanging on to Oscar's leash, Matthew struggled to keep up with Luke, who carried a bag of Dog Chow on his shoulder. At the Explorer, Luke opened the rear hatch and tossed the dog food inside.

"The hardware store." Luke slammed the hatch and herded boy and dog around to the door of the vehicle. "Hop in."

"Okay." Handing over the leash, the boy climbed into the front seat with a boost from Luke and scrambled over the console to the passenger's side.

"Buckle up," Luke told him, watching to see that he did. Oscar, meanwhile, leaped to the center of the back seat and sat on his haunches.

"Where's the hardware store?" Matthew asked.

"Not far from here," Luke said.

The kid asked a million questions. Luke had been sharing baby-sitting duty for three days along with Chloe Blackwell, but she'd be going back to college at the first of the year. Surely there would have been some word from Phyllis by then.

"Can Keely find us there?"

"You bet."

No psychiatrist was needed to figure out where Matthew was coming from on that one. He'd transferred his dependence on his mother to Keely. He wanted to be reassured about Keely. He asked often how long till Keely got home, or if Keely knew

Luke's phone number, or would Keely worry if she got home and he wasn't there. Keely might eventually persuade the Barlows to take him, but Luke was convinced Matthew wouldn't willingly be parted from her.

It still baffled Luke how he'd gotten himself involved in this. Sure, he was concerned about Laura and Randall, but he didn't think either of them would commit to something as important as taking in a little kid if there were compelling reasons not to. So they didn't need his input to hold Keely off. Actually, it was him, not his aunt and uncle, who could use some protection against Keely. As a second-year resident, he worked a killer schedule—mostly thirty-six hours on and only twenty-four off before he was back at the hospital. Any spare time he usually guarded jealously. There wasn't room in his life to baby-sit a four-year-old.

"Look, they got a lot of Christmas trees over there!" Matthew's nose was pressed to the side window, surveying the huge lot roped off in the center of the parking area.

"Yeah, but Keely's already got a Christmas tree." Luke started the Explorer and began backing out.

Matthew turned toward Luke. "But you need one, don'tcha, Luke?"

No, he didn't for at least a dozen reasons. But at the look on the boy's face, all Luke's excuses seemed lame. "My place is pretty crowded," he said weakly. "And I don't have any decorations. So I was planning to skip this year." The truth was he never put up a tree.

"Oh." Matthew turned his gaze back to the window. "Billy busted all our decorations. That's why we're skipping this year."

Damn. Luke drove past the Christmas trees. "How'd that happen?"

Matthew watched a family trying to choose a tree—two boys, early grammar school age and a smaller girl, with mom and dad. "He got mad when Mommy started unpacking the box and he kicked it and everything in it was all busted up."

"Everything?" Luke was finding it hard to think of a punishment bad enough for Billy Long.

Matthew was nodding. "Even the star that went on top."

"I tell you what." Luke pulled up beside a pickup truck and stopped the Explorer. "Now that I think about it, that corner where I keep my golf clubs is about right for a Christmas tree. We could pick one out now and stop in at Target and get some lights and balls and…whatever else you think we might need."

Matthew looked at him in unabashed delight. "Oh, wow!" Sensing Matthew's joy, Oscar gave a hearty woof.

"Well, what are we waiting for?" Luke found himself grinning. "Let's do it!"

"All right!" Matthew laughed, dodging Oscar, who was enthusiastically licking his face.

What the hell. Luke walked around to the passenger side and waited for the boy to scramble out with the dog. While Matthew dashed about looking at trees, Oscar trotted by his side. Standing at the roped-off lot, Luke watched the young family now piling into the pickup. Dad had loaded the tree into the back with a lot of help from the two boys. Driving away, he met Luke's eyes and gave him a rueful grin. For a moment, Luke almost felt a kinship. And a flash of envy. It was the envy that unnerved him. His gaze wandered to Matthew, scurrying from tree to tree trying to make a choice. Too bad Keely was missing this moment.

"This is the best one!" Matthew finally declared, gazing up at a twenty-foot blue spruce that would have fit nicely in the lobby of a bank.

Luke steered him away from the giant and after an exhaustive search, they finally settled on a six-foot tree with branches that would probably obstruct the view of his television, but football season was almost over anyway.

What the hell.

"Next Christmas can we get a bigger one?" Matthew asked, trudging along beside Luke as they headed for the Explorer.

Luke pulled the hatch open and shoved the tree inside. "I don't see why not."

"But what if Billy gets mad and I don't get to have a tree next Christmas?"

Luke closed the hatch and squatted to look the boy straight in the eye. "I promise you, Matthew, you will never have to spend another Christmas with Billy Long."

CHAPTER FIVE

KEELY KNEW SOMEONE WAS in the apartment the moment she stepped inside. Which surprised her because Matthew and Luke were supposed to be decorating the tree at his place. Amazing that Luke was even getting a tree, but more amazing that he'd found somebody to take his shift at the hospital!

"Hello, I'm home!" She felt a little leap of pleasure. One of the nicest things about having Matthew around was the warm welcome she got upon opening the door. It wasn't only Matthew, of course, it was Luke, too. But she wasn't ready to admit that Luke contributed as much to her pleasure as Matthew. As she tossed her handbag onto a chair, she thought a muffled sound came from somewhere in the back of the apartment.

"Hey, where are you two?"

There was no denying her attraction to Luke, even though she'd been careful not to reveal it. What had started out as a simple effort by the two of them to share responsibility for Matthew until his mom returned was beginning to feel more complicated. She wasn't sure what she wanted to do about it yet.

Shedding her coat, she moved to the thermostat to take some of the chill off. Why was it the males of the species were never as vulnerable to cold? She hoped Luke had thought to bundle Matthew up warmly when they went to get dog food. He wasn't used to having the care of a child and the last thing they needed was for Matthew to get sick.

Kicking off her shoes, she padded down the hall wondering where they were and thinking that at least Oscar could have come out to greet her. But with Matthew's arrival she was now second-best in Oscar's life. Or at least she hoped she was still second. Like Matthew, Oscar was falling in love with Luke, too.

First Matthew, then Oscar. Three's a charm.

Silly thought. She might be liking the man better and she might be seeing a few—just a few—qualities in him that could bear exploring in her spare time—provided she had any spare time—but she wasn't falling in love with Luke Jamison. Hard, unemotional, chauvinistic. Who needed it?

"Hey! Doesn't anybody care that I'm home?"

Silence. Disappointed, she realized nobody was here. Her first impression had been wrong.

Frowning, she wandered down the hall. *Brr!* Her bedroom was freezing! And with good reason, she discovered with an irritable huff, somebody had

left one of the French doors open. She pulled it
shut and locked it securely. Matthew must have
been playing on the patio and forgotten to close it.
She'd have to remind Luke to check the doors and
windows when they left to be sure everything was
secured. She wasn't the nervous type, but she
wasn't reckless, either. Every apartment complex
had its share of strange tenants. She didn't want to
leave an open invitation to one of them.

Glancing at the clock, she decided to take time
to change into jeans and a fisherman-knit sweater
before going to Luke's place. Since they'd teamed
up to take care of Matthew, they'd fallen into a
fairly workable system, with the help of Chloe
Blackwell. On the days Luke was able to help and
their schedules meshed, he and Matthew waited for
Keely in her apartment after which he hustled off
to the hospital. Even though they'd gone along
fairly smoothly for over a week, both of them
knew they were going to have to make more permanent plans. Keely hadn't a clue what those plans
might be.

Bundled up again a few minutes later, she
dashed across the lawn between her building and
Luke's and arrived breathless and chilled at his
door. Matthew let her in.

"Come see, Keely! Come see!" Not giving her
a chance to shed her coat, he pulled her into the
living room. She stopped short. There had been no

Christmas tree here the last time she looked. Now one stood proudly in the corner amidst empty ornament boxes and all manner of torn wrapping. Not to mention the trail of dry needles littering the carpet.

''Whoa! That's some tree you've got there.'' She met Luke's sheepish gaze and grinned. Apparently he wasn't the only one who was putty in Matthew's small hands.

''You should see the one we passed up,'' he muttered.

Matthew was dancing with excitement. ''Me and Luke've been working hard to decorate it before you got home!''

''And you've done a fabulous job,'' she told him, squeezing his hand. Again she looked at Luke. ''Working hard, you say?''

Luke saluted her with a beer, one eyebrow arched.

''We put an angel on top of it,'' Matthew said.

Standing on tiptoe, Keely solemnly examined the angel. ''Ohh, nice. How did you ever find such a beautiful angel, Matthew?''

The little boy sighed as if it had been a truly exhausting quest. ''We just did our best. She has her own box and everything to keep her safe for next year.'' He paused for a moment. ''I'm going to be here with you and Luke next Christmas, not with Billy.'' Confidently he added, ''Luke said.''

"THAT'S NOT WHAT I SAID. Not exactly." With a harried look on his face, Luke stood watching Keely pull wrapping paper and Scotch tape out of a shopping bag. Matthew had fallen asleep after dinner and was now out like a light in Luke's guest room, so she'd decided to wrap a couple of things here. "Hell, I'd like to promise him a lot more than that. God knows, the world owes him a Christmas without the fear that Billy will show up and ruin everything. But I didn't promise he'd spend Christmas with you and me."

Keely cut a long length of bright red paper to fit a box of Lego. "Well, if Phyllis doesn't show up, it's a good bet he'll spend this Christmas with us—or with me if you have plans. But you're right not to promise more than you can deliver. Matthew's had too many promises made to him and then broken."

"I don't have plans," Luke said.

"I'm not sure what I'll do, but whatever comes up, Matthew's included."

Now pacing, Luke continued, "This is getting pretty complicated, Keely."

She reached for tape. "What is?"

"Our...arrangement." He waved a hand at the tree. "Having a kid around is like being a little bit pregnant. There's no such thing. Shouldn't he be in kindergarten or something?"

"Some kids are in pre-K at Matthew's age, but

apparently he wasn't. I agree we'll have to do something soon, but under the circumstances, I thought we'd wait until we heard from Phyllis. Surely she'll call soon.''

Luke was silent for a moment as she tied bright ribbon around the box. ''The longer Phyllis is absent, the more dependent on you he'll become.''

She looked up at him. ''And you.''

''We're going to have to come up with a better plan.''

Keely found a name tag and wrote Matthew's name on it. He was right to push on this, of course. Luke had already done more than she'd ever dreamed he would for Matthew's sake. But she kept hoping the Barlows would come through. Randall had asked about Matthew today, but he hadn't volunteered anything. She assumed Laura was still unwilling.

She sighed and leaned back. ''Have you got any suggestions? I'm fresh out.''

''Foster care is not an option. There are probably good people out there, but I'm not willing to take a chance.''

She smiled. ''I'm glad you're making progress.''

''I'll try to see my aunt tomorrow.''

Keely's eyes widened. ''What brought on this change of heart? I thought Laura Barlow's welfare outweighed any needs of an abandoned four-year-old.''

"You said Phyllis hadn't abandoned Matthew."

"She didn't. She—"

"Had no choice," he finished for her.

"That's right."

Luke sank onto the couch. "I'm going to take him with me when I go. He's cute, and he's smart. I mean, he's...entertaining." Shaking his head, he studied the label on his beer. "He comes up with some amazing stuff. Matthew himself is the best argument I can come up with for trying to bring her around. She might actually enjoy him."

"Sounds as if you do."

"Yeah."

She slipped the package into a large shopping bag and grinned. "Join the club."

"You know what he told me? They couldn't have a tree this year. That bastard Billy went nuts and destroyed the decorations! No kid should have to live with that memory."

"Better the memory than the reality." From the bar, she lifted a mug, warm with spiced tea, and went over to the sofa, settling in the corner and tucking her feet beneath her. "So, it's going pretty well between you two?"

"We do okay."

Smiling, Keely looked at the Christmas tree, twinkling with a hundred tiny lights, but lopsided in the placement of ornaments. "I don't think I've ever seen Christmas balls in a *Star Wars* motif."

"Better than *The Simpsons* or *Rugrats*."

She laughed. "I have a bunch of stuff I didn't use this year. If you'd asked, I would have told you where to find it. Oh, that reminds me." Leaning forward, she put her tea on the coffee table. "Did you know Matthew left the patio door open in my bedroom? The apartment was cold as a meat locker when I got home."

He was frowning. "We put Oscar's dog food in the kitchen pantry and came straight back here. Matthew was in my sight the whole time."

"My bedroom..." Her voice trailed off. "I know it was locked when I left this morning. I would never leave it open. Besides, it's too cold. I would have—"

"Good Lord, Keely. Somebody broke into your house and you're just now thinking to mention it?" He stood up. "How do you know he wasn't inside waiting? How do you know he isn't waiting for you right now?"

"Wait a minute! Aren't you jumping to a pretty rash conclusion? There's probably a reason my door was ajar."

"Name one."

"Well..."

He tossed his beer bottle into a trash can. "Great, this is all we need."

She put a hand on her throat. "I thought it was

you," she murmured. Her heart was beginning to race.

"Well, it wasn't. We need to call the cops, get somebody out here to check it out. They can question tenants to see if anybody noticed a stranger or anything out of the ordinary. We need to—"

"Wait, wait…" She put up a hand. "I need to go back and check to see if anything's been disturbed or…or whatever. I didn't notice anything when I came in, but thinking back, I did hear a sound. I thought it was you and Matthew. I called out—"

"Announcing that you were home and alone." His tone was harsh.

Stung, Keely shot back. "Are you saying I was careless because I unlocked the door of my own apartment and went inside before sweeping the place for intruders? Or was I just dumb?"

"That's not what I'm saying. I'm just—" He looked at her as if searching for words. "Hell, it just scares me to think that you surprised some lowlife. He ran…this time. But what if he hadn't?"

"You're doing it again, Luke," she told him in a warning tone. "Didn't we have this conversation when Billy Long tried bullying me in the waiting room? I've been on my own for quite some time. Trust me, I can take care of myself."

"How?" Luke knew he was on shaky ground— she was one independent lady—but he'd seen the flash of fear when she'd realized a stranger could have been in her apartment waiting for her. "Just how would you do that?"

Unintimidated, she said, "I've had some training in self-defense." Then before she could even blink, he hauled her up and locked his arms around her. "Hey!"

"Show me," he said, his nose almost touching hers. "Defend yourself. I've surprised you in your house. I waited until you came into your bedroom and I grabbed you." He gave a little thrust of his pelvis just to ruffle her. "And I'm liking the way you feel."

She began to push and shove against him. "Let me go!"

"Telling some scumbag who's got the hots for you to 'let go' won't do it, darlin'."

She almost managed, with a swift twist, to lift her knee and deliver the classic defense, but he was ready. Fending her off with a soft laugh, he said, "You'll have to do better, sweetheart. He'll be on guard for that one."

Keely drew in a sharp breath as he gently bit her neck. "Come on, Luke…" She made a small sound as he went a little further, nuzzling her ear. "I… You…you've made your point."

But he wasn't listening. Now that he'd had the first taste of her, he found himself losing the urge to teach her a lesson. He began raining kisses over her cheeks and nose and eyes. Pleased, he felt the fight go out of her. Unresisting...

"So stop me," he breathed, pausing at the corner of her mouth.

She made a little sound, a soft whisper of need, and with it, Luke felt a mindless rush take over his head, his body, his senses. And then his mouth was on hers, hungry and urgent. He gathered her close, exulting in the taste of her, in the warmth and softness of her.

He was wild with the scent of her, the feel of her as she responded to him. He'd imagined a million times what Keely would be like and it was better, a thousand times better than any of his fantasies.

He pulled her over to the sofa, taking her down in a tangle of limbs and covering her body with his own. Shoving the sweater up, he found she wore no bra and blessed the impulse that had made her leave it off. Her breasts were small and satin smooth to his touch. She whimpered when he rubbed his thumbs over the sensitive tips, throwing her head back and offering a feast for his senses. He took a breast into his mouth and groaned when she wrapped her long legs around his middle, warming him with the heated heart of her.

Keely was stunned at the overload of sensation gripping her. His mouth was hot at her breast, calling up an urgent, compelling response from deep inside. Now he was kissing her stomach, moving lower still, unimpeded by her waistband, to her navel. She cried out as his tongue dipped and swirled. He'd made his point. He was stronger and he could overpower her, but with his mouth all over and his hands working such magic, she didn't care about any of that. Everything he did felt wonderful. With every move, she was pushed to the next level until she was a seething mass of need. She just wanted more. And more.

Her response shocked her. She'd always preferred a gentle lover, a man with patience and a slow hand. But when Luke's fingers began to work at the snap of her jeans, she lifted her hips in an eager rush to help, greedy, mindless and readied for the fullness of completion.

Then the telephone rang.

He went taut and still. His hands at her waist flexed a little too hard, drawing a small wince from her. Resting his forehead on her belly, he breathed like a man finishing a brutal run. "Not now... *damn it!*"

"We...we have to," she said, staring up at the ceiling and feeling disoriented. Another ring. Both knew it could be the hospital. Keely was on call. "I left this number," she told him.

She was still imprisoned by his body and strangely reluctant to move. The third ring. And the fourth. Sitting up, he reached to pull down her sweater. "You can get it," he said, motioning to the telephone on the end table closest to her.

Keely lifted the receiver and was startled to hear Randall Barlow's voice. "Keely! Have I dialed the wrong number?"

"No, no. I'm— Did you want Luke?"

"You'll want to hear this, too." Randall paused. "Is the boy still with you?"

"Matthew? Yes, of course."

"I've just received a call from Roanoke, Virginia, about Phyllis Long."

"Phyllis is in Virginia?" Keely met Luke's dark gaze and covered the mouthpiece. "It's Randall."

"They called the hospital and the chaplain on duty called me," Randall continued. "She had the discharge papers from the E.R. among her things."

"Among her things?" Keely's breath stopped.

Seeing her face, Luke rose and reached for the receiver. "What is it?"

But she was shaking her head. "Randall, is she okay?"

"I'm afraid not, Keely. She's been murdered."

CHAPTER SIX

LUKE WALKED DOWN THE HALL to the bedroom where Matthew slept and quietly closed the door. Without looking at Keely, he went to the fridge and got a beer. On the kitchen table lay a collection of small ornaments—a carved Santa with his reindeer—that Matthew had been playing with before going to bed. Luke touched Rudolph, making a tiny bell tinkle. "Merry Christmas, Matt," he muttered.

"How will we tell him?" Keely asked in a worried tone. She was still trying to take it in herself. In spite of her concern for Phyllis's safety, she hadn't been prepared for anything like murder.

"I don't know." Luke sat down on the couch, dangling his beer between his knees. "But however it's done, I think we should wait until morning."

He was right, of course. There was no need to wake Matthew to tell him his mother was dead. Let his childhood last another twelve hours. The unfairness of it all brought her up from the couch to pace around the room.

"It was Billy, wasn't it, Luke? Somehow he found her and killed her."

"At the moment he seems to be the prime suspect. Homicide in Roanoke has an APB out for him."

She stopped, giving him a sharp look. "Did Randall tell you that?"

Luke had taken the phone after Randall had told Keely about Phyllis. In her shock, Keely had missed some of the conversation.

"There wasn't much to tell. Just that once they'd identified Phyllis and learned there was a history of abuse, they naturally focused on her estranged husband. Their judgment is borne out by statistics. Too often the guilty party is someone close, a family member."

"Guilty party." Keely's face wrinkled with distaste. "That's too tame a description for an animal like Billy Long."

"Yeah. And we have to keep in mind that he is an animal and that he's dangerous. So until he's behind bars, we've got another problem."

Keely frowned. "What problem?"

"Phyllis's body was discovered around midday, but a detective told Randall she'd been dead almost twenty-four hours. If it was Billy, he's had time to travel from Roanoke to Atlanta, easy."

Keely's heart dipped. "Meaning he could be here."

"And he could be looking for Matthew."

"That would be so stupid!" Keely said, appalled—and scared—at the very thought. "He's not even Matthew's natural father. Phyllis made certain I knew that when she left him with me. So why would Billy want him?"

"Why would he kill his wife? Don't make the mistake of thinking you can get inside the head of a man like Billy Long. Or that murdering his wife is the worst thing he can do."

Keely's imagination was busy filling in the details. Not Matthew. Billy wouldn't hurt Matthew, would he? "Only someone who's crazy would come after Matthew now," she murmured.

"Or crazy mean. Whatever, we won't assume he's stupid. Which is the reason we have to make sure he doesn't get close to Matthew." Getting up, Luke moved to the front window and cracked a blind so he could see outside. "If he isn't already close."

Keely felt a chill run down her spine. "You don't see anything, do you?" she asked, moving to his side. Security lights illuminated the cars parked in the complex. Nothing moved. But, if he were skulking around at midnight in a complex with tight security, he'd be careful not to be seen, wouldn't he?

Luke dropped the blind. "No, but that doesn't mean he isn't out there."

For a long moment, Keely stared into his eyes. "Do you honestly think he might come after Matthew?"

"I don't have a clue." Without finishing his beer, Luke set the bottle on an end table nearby. "But somebody was in your apartment today. Until we know who it was, and why, we can't take any chances."

"I don't plan to take any chances."

He gave a skeptical grunt.

"I'm not an idiot, Luke!"

"Good. Because it's late and I don't want to waste more time arguing. We've got two things to decide. One is where you and Matthew are going to spend the night. Second is what we're going to do about Matthew tomorrow and for however long it takes the cops to find Billy." He held up a hand. "Before you blow a gasket, just listen. We were able to take care of Matthew without help because temporarily our schedules meshed well. But in a couple of days our schedules change. We need to think about day care."

"We? Does this mean you're still committed?"

"Do I have any choice?"

She was suddenly furious. Furious and scared. "Absolutely! If you want to walk away now, just say the word. Matthew has always been my responsibility. I promised his mother and…and…"

"And now that he doesn't have a mother, you're ready to step into that role completely."

"Yes!" she cried. "Damn right." Even though she wasn't certain at all that she was prepared—or capable—of being Matthew's mother.

He sighed with impatience. "What's the point in all this, Keely? We're stuck with—"

"*We're* not stuck with anything!" she said. "Matthew's not an…an inconvenience like a head cold or a…a flat tire. He's a little boy and he's lost his mother and she…sh-she's counting on me to bring him through this. And without destroying his faith in people for the rest of his life, too!" She blinked tears back as her voice caught. "S-so now that the situation's getting a little sticky, if you want to bail out on him, then go ahead! We'll manage, just Matthew and me!"

"Are you finished?"

Eyes wet, her chin went up pugnaciously. "It depends."

Wearily he clamped a hand on the back of his neck. "I'm not walking away, Keely. I'm trying to point out the problems we're facing. As long as Billy is somewhere out there, Matthew isn't just some other little kid who's in danger of falling through the cracks of a bureaucratic system. He could be Billy's next victim. It's up to us to safeguard him." Again he put up a hand to stop her. "One more thing—we don't know that he's after

Matthew. *You* could be the object of his obsession.''

"Me?"

"Without your help, Phyllis might not have been able to run. I'm not saying that's the way Billy's looking at it, but I don't want to take a chance until the guy's apprehended.''

"And I think you're overreacting." She could see Luke visibly controlling his exasperation. She shivered a little at the thought, not of Luke losing control, but of the passion that could erupt between them if he did. Again. Later she'd think about the odd compulsion that made her want to provoke him.

She sighed. "Look, I understand the danger to Matthew. I'm not about to take foolish chances. I was surviving on the streets of New Orleans when I was fourteen years old. Do you think I made it by disregarding basic common sense?''

Almost growling, he drove the fingers of one hand through his hair. "I don't know how you did it then. I'm just urging caution for now.''

She waved a hand. "Then relax. Consider me properly cautioned.''

He was silent a beat or two. "Are you deliberately trying to rile me?''

Tension radiated from him. He was so close that she could almost feel the vibrations. The memory of those moments on the couch rose suddenly between them. For Keely, it was like a rush of warm honey throughout her whole body. She almost wished that she could just step into his arms and let him assume the responsibility for Matthew and this crazy, awful situation, but that was a spineless attitude. Besides, it was she, not Luke, who'd promised Phyllis.

She put a hand to her forehead. "I'm sorry. I know I sound...contrary."

He nearly smiled. "Yeah. You also sound like a worried mom."

Her throat tightened. She bent down and picked up two small sneakers on the floor. Holding them against her heart, she looked at him. "You're right about day care. In fact, I was planning to talk to you about it. Chloe worked in the child-care center at St. Dominic's in the summer. The place has a good reputation and there's excellent security, too. I didn't mention it before because I was hoping Phyllis would return and Matthew wouldn't have to cope with more change. But it looks as if change can't be avoided."

"We can try Randall and Laura again tomorrow," Luke said, but Keely could tell that he wasn't expecting much there. Because her throat was dry and her eyes burned, she set the sneakers gently on the coffee table and turned away.

"How much can a little boy take, Luke?"

He shrugged helplessly. "I'm way out of my

league on the emotional stuff, you know that. But keeping him—and you—safe until the threat of Billy Long is past is something I'm ready and able to do.''

"How? You're in the middle of your residency, Luke. What can you do?''

"I didn't plan to get involved, but whether I planned it or not, I *am* involved. Look, I need you to trust me on this, Keely. I was in Intelligence in the Army. Intelligence and law enforcement go hand in hand. This situation is shaping up to look more and more risky—for Matthew and for you.''

"Maybe, but still…what can you do?''

"For starters, you can spend the night here. We can't take the chance that Billy might show up again at your apartment.''

"We don't know it was Billy.'' But there was doubt in her voice. Could she take a chance with Matthew's safety at stake? That skirmish with Luke proved she could be overwhelmed by a determined man.

Luke went over to the door and unlocked it. "We have to assume it was Billy. I don't even want to take a chance on you running across to your place to get your things. Tell me what you need and I'll go get it.''

"Wait.'' She glanced down the hall. There were only two bedrooms, Luke's and the guest room where Matthew slept. "I'm not sleeping with you, Luke."

"No, not yet." But something in his eyes made her heart do a flip. "Tonight you can share with Matthew."

"Pajamas," she said, the word coming out in a rush. Wow, give Luke Jamison an inch and he grabbed a mile! "In the second drawer of my armoire. Makeup kit is hanging behind the bathroom door. I keep it stocked and ready so I won't have to bother every time I want to sleep over somewhere."

His mouth tilted in a slow smile. "And are you in the habit of doing that often?"

"Yes," she said, squaring her shoulders and managing at last to get a grip. "When I'm on duty at the hospital."

CHAPTER SEVEN

UNTIL THE DAY HIS DAUGHTER DIED, Randall Barlow's life as a minister had been remarkably peaceful and blessed. Before accepting the position as chaplain at St. Dominic's, he'd pastored several churches in towns where he and his wife were warmly received and where his role as a man of God was revered and respected. At times he'd felt a fraud. There were secrets in his past that haunted him, but for the most part he'd managed to keep his personal demons under control and out of sight. Or at least only partially—and rarely—visible.

The move to St. Dominic's had been as much for Laura's sake as for his own. He'd sensed her weariness with the ceaseless demands of a congregation. So, in a way, the move had been like a semi-retirement for them. But then Shelley had died. It had been a good thing that he wasn't pastoring a church, as he simply hadn't had enough spiritual energy left to "shepherd a flock." At the hospital, there was less chance of getting deeply involved in the lives of people. His exposure to individuals in turmoil at St. Dominic's was just one small snapshot in time compared to the ongoing relationship he'd been forced to maintain as a pastor. Generally the patients and their loved ones moved on and he turned his attention to the next.

But Phyllis Long had been different. Something about the woman had touched him. Maybe he might have succeeded in pushing her and her predicament into that guarded place in his mind, except for Keely's fierce lobbying on behalf of the woman's little boy, not to mention Luke's surprising interest. Now he was beginning to wonder if distancing himself from Matthew was going to be possible.

And, deep down, did he really want to turn away?

"Randall? Dinner's ready." Laura came into the den, wiping her hands on a terry tea towel. "What has you so distracted, for heaven's sake? I've called you several times!"

His wife was an excellent cook. You wouldn't guess by looking at her in her smart butterscotch-colored knitted sweater and cream wool slacks that she'd probably produced from scratch a meal fit for company. Her hair, recently highlighted by her favorite stylist, was cut in the Diane Sawyer fashion she favored and unmussed from her efforts in the kitchen. She looked lovely and pampered, cool and fresh.

Randall put aside the newspaper. "I was just reading about the murder of Phyllis Long."

Laura's expression cooled. "I don't know why some women make the choices they do."

"I doubt that Phyllis knew Billy would turn out to be violent when they first met," Randall said dryly.

"Maybe not, but after he showed those tendencies, there's no excuse for staying with him."

"She's not so different from many women in abusive relationships." Randall stood up, following as his wife led the way to the dining room. "And when we figure out why they stay, we'll save a lot of grief in the world."

He waited until Laura was seated at the table, then pulled out his own chair and sat down. After spreading his napkin, he picked up his fork. "Everything has changed with the death of the boy's mother. You realize that, don't you, Laura?"

"Of course. A permanent home will have to be found. I hope there are relatives."

"No. At least the police haven't located anyone."

Laura cut delicately into a medallion of succulent pork. "I'll make some calls tomorrow. As I mentioned when we discussed this earlier, there are agencies. The boy's situation boosts him high on the adoption list. And since he's so young, there's no doubt someone will snap him up."

Randall rested both hands on the table edge. "You make him sound like a puppy."

"Randall…" She took a sip of water. "Let's not discuss this right now, please."

"Fine. When exactly can we discuss it?"

She made a small sound. "Why do we have to discuss it at all? We have no responsibility in situations like this anymore. You're a hospital chaplain now, not the pastor of a church. Phyllis Long was not your parishioner."

"She meant the boy to be left in my care, Laura. I can't just dismiss that. It's a more compelling responsibility than if she'd been just a parishioner."

Laura sighed. "Has that…Dr. Hamilton…has she been at you again?"

Randall looked up from his plate. "At me? Keely? In what way?"

Her mouth twisted. "I wish you wouldn't call her by her first name. Do you think it's appropriate?"

"I call most of the residents at St. Dominic's by their first names. Besides, she's been to our home. She asked you to call her Keely."

"Well then…" She took up her knife and fork again. "Did *Keely* ask you to reconsider? I'll tell you right now, Randall, that I think it's very… pushy of her to keep on with this."

"She's acting out of concern for the boy."

Laura studied him suspiciously. "You did refuse her, didn't you? You told her we couldn't take the boy, even temporarily, didn't you?"

"She knows that decision must come from both of us."

"So she *has* been at you again!"

"Laura—"

With a clink of silver, Laura abruptly rose from her chair. Her chin was up and her tone was cold as she spoke. "I don't want to hear any more. If you keep pressuring me about this, I can only assume that my feelings are less important than someone else's." She dropped her napkin. "I've lost my appetite."

"Wait, Laura."

Laura was surprised when Randall caught her wrist as she started past him. After twenty-four years of marriage, she felt she knew her husband very well. Randall was slow to anger, but he was angry now. And there was something else in his expression, a look that made her feel uncomfortable somehow.

"Sit back down," he said in a quiet voice. "Walking off will only prolong this dilemma."

"*What* dilemma!" Her heartbeat was fast and furious. "We've discussed it and the answer's no."

"That's *your* decision, Laura. Not mine."

Now she was angry. "Are you telling me that I can't refuse to go along with this crazy scheme?"

"Crazy? Why is it crazy to temporarily open our home to a little boy whose mother has been murdered?"

"My daughter was murdered!" Laura cried, suddenly losing all composure. *"Have you forgotten that?"*

"Shelley was not murdered. She died in a car accident. But even so, how does that justify closing our hearts to Matthew just now when he's so desperately in need?"

"There's no place in my heart for any other child, Randall," she said in a tone vibrating with emotion. "No matter how needy or how desperate. What will it take to convince you?"

An endless moment passed. Obviously realizing he still held her wrist, Randall let go. "I promised I'd try once more, but I can see you're in no frame of mind to listen right now."

"I knew it!"

He gave a weary sigh. "Knew what?"

"That she was behind this. That it was her idea. You ignore what I think while doing everything you can to please her!"

"You're referring to Keely?"

"You *know* I am!"

"Actually, it was Luke, not Keely, who approached me this morning after we'd broken the news to the boy that his mother was gone," he told her as he rose. "Not that it matters which one it was. Once I learned about Phyllis, I knew I had to try again to change your mind. Luke and Keely have been caring for Matthew together and doing an incredible job, I might add, but it's strictly a temporary arrangement. They both have demanding schedules and something has to give. The boy needs a real home with a loving couple." He put his napkin on the table. There was disappointment and regret in his voice. "You can relax now, Laura. That doesn't describe us, does it?"

THERE HAD BEEN TOO MANY TIMES as a physician when Keely had had to tell a family member that someone near and dear had died. But never had it been as heart wrenching as telling Matthew. There was simply no good way—certainly no easy way—to explain to a four-year-old boy that his mother was gone forever. That in spite of her promise to return, she never would.

Keely had insisted on Luke and Randall being with her. She wanted Matthew to have all the support he could possibly want or need. But to her surprise when they finally managed to tell him, it was to Keely that Matthew had turned, throwing his arms around her neck and sobbing his heart out.

"Where's Billy?" he'd asked after the storm of tears was over. No one had mentioned his stepfather or the manner of Phyllis's death, but Matthew was clearly fearful that Long might appear. Safe in Keely's lap, his gaze had gone to Luke for reassurance.

"Don't worry about Billy," Luke had told him. "The police are looking for him. They'll find him soon."

"I don't want to go live with him." Matthew had pressed closer to Keely.

"You won't have to live with Billy." Keely's arms had tightened around him fiercely. "I promise."

But still Matthew had been leery. He'd watched the windows in Randall's office fearfully, as if expecting to see his stepfather appear. It wasn't going to be easy to convince Matthew that Billy wouldn't pop up and create more misery in his life. Until he got used to his changed circumstances, he was going to need constant reassurance. Day care, of course, looked even more certain now, but Keely worried about leaving him there. She and Luke worked long, sometimes erratic hours and if Laura Barlow, who was in the most favorable position to help out, didn't come around soon, Keely was afraid the courts might decide to step in. She couldn't let that happen.

FOR THE SECOND TIME in ten days, Keely found herself at the Barlows' pretty house. It had taken some creative shuffling of the duty roster to get away in the middle of the day, but she simply couldn't ignore the urgency of finding the right place for Matthew. Thank God for Chloe Blackwell and her willingness to step in when Keely and Luke, who was in the middle of a thirty-six hour shift, were both working. But Chloe was going back to school after the New Year.

Praying that her purpose in visiting Laura Barlow did not fail, Keely got out of her car and headed up the neat sidewalk.

This time, she didn't have Luke to ease any awkwardness. Or a sweet little boy to personally plead his own case. Even if she'd asked Luke, he probably would have refused. He was convinced, after talking to Randall, that Laura was not going to change her mind. Keely was unwilling to accept that until she made one last attempt for Matthew's sake.

After ringing the bell, she stood for a moment looking directly into the peephole and wondered what she'd do if Laura Barlow wouldn't even hear her out. But no, a minister's wife wouldn't be that hard-hearted, would she?

Laura Barlow opened the door wearing a too-cool, too-polite look of inquiry. "Dr. Hamilton."

Dr. Hamilton. Back to formality, Keely thought. It didn't bode well for the purpose of her visit. "Hello," she said.

"Were you looking for my husband?"

"Ah, no. Actually…" Keely managed a smile even though there was no welcome in the woman's expression "…it was you I wanted to see." Keely could have been a total stranger. Even though she hadn't expected gushing warmth, neither had she expected near-hostility. "Do you have a minute to talk?"

Laura glanced at her watch. "Is it important?"

She was going to refuse, Keely thought with dismay. Had they all been pushing too hard? Had they all been so focused on Matthew and his needs that they'd alienated the best and last chance for him? But then, to Keely's relief, Laura stepped back, holding the door until she was inside.

"Thanks," Keely said, looking around appreciatively at the festively decorated foyer and realizing, from Laura's distant reception, that she was unlikely to get beyond it. Chatting in the cozy family room where she, Luke and the Barlows had first discussed Matthew's fate wasn't on the agenda today. With a mental shrug, she dismissed the snub as unimportant. "It's about Matthew," she told Randall's wife.

"We can talk in here," Laura said, turning and heading for the arched entry to a formal living room.

Keely followed her and took the seat Laura offered, a beautiful floral wing chair. Laura sat opposite her on the edge of a Victorian sofa, ramrod straight. Centered on the coffee table between them was a gorgeous red poinsettia on a pedestal. A barrier? Keely wondered. A line in the sand? This was not shaping up to be a friendly talk.

"You know about Phyllis Long, of course," Keely said, getting to the point quickly.

"I know she died, yes."

"She was murdered, Mrs. Barlow."

Laura looked past Keely to a window. "There seems to be more and more violence in the world today."

"Tell me about it." The E.R. certainly kept Keely grounded. "There are two victims here, Mrs. Barlow. Matthew is as much a victim as his mother."

"Yes," she said. "Randall and I were discussing it last night at dinner."

"We're very concerned about Matthew."

"It's wise not to get too close in these matters."

"Too late," Keely said, trying not to be offended to hear Matthew's situation characterized in such a bloodless way. "Matthew sneaked into my heart about ten minutes after we met." Keely smiled. "It took a little longer to win Luke over. Like maybe…thirty minutes."

"Yes, I understand the two of you are sharing custody, so to speak." Her gaze rested for a moment on Keely. "Amazing, really."

"That we've become so attached to Matthew? He's adorable. Smart, funny—"

"Actually, I meant it was amazing that Luke was getting so involved. He's never shown much interest in children. Just look at the specialty he's considering—trauma medicine."

Keely knew Luke was seriously considering surgery as a specialty, but she said nothing to contradict his aunt. "He didn't seem to have much trouble connecting with Matthew. They're tight."

"What was it you wanted to talk to me about, Dr. Hamilton?"

Keely drew in a breath. "Mrs. Barlow, no matter how much Luke and I love Matthew, we can't continue as we've been doing. Shuffling from my place to Luke's is unfair and unsettling, especially now. He needs stability. Security. He needs two loving parents, a mom and a dad."

"I completely agree. I said as much to Randall last night."

"But you don't see yourself and Ran—Dr. Barlow volunteering to fulfill that need?"

"There are other ways that Randall and I choose to contribute to the welfare of displaced children."

"And I'm sure those projects are worthwhile, but...forgive me, I just feel Dr. Barlow might have some special feelings for Matthew. Maybe it's because Phyllis particularly asked that—"

Laura rose abruptly. "She had no right to make

such a request. My husband is a minister, but that doesn't mean people can impose burdens upon him they'd never dream of asking of others. Doctors, for example,'' she added with some bitterness.

"I know Phyllis thought it would be temporary,'' Keely said. "She couldn't have anticipated her own murder.''

"Actually, I think she did suspect she would meet with violence at the hand of her husband,'' Laura said coolly. "Why didn't she leave him years ago? It is she who has jeopardized her son's future, not I.''

Keely took a slow breath. It couldn't get any plainer than that, but she found herself making one more stab at opening this woman's heart. "And you're confident that Randall...Dr. Barlow is going to be comfortable with your decision?''

"Yes.'' Laura turned to look at her, adding, "Unless you're suggesting that you know something about my husband's feelings on this subject that he hasn't shared with me?''

"Of course not,'' Keely said, appalled at the very thought. "It's just that I've heard Dr. Barlow talking about Matthew, recalling Phyllis's concern about him that night in the E.R., which was only a short time before she was murdered.''

"The whole situation is extremely unfortunate,'' Laura said, flicking at a speck of lint on the sleeve of her blazer. "But there are agencies...''

"Unfortunate." Keely repeated the word, realizing it left a bad taste in her mouth. "Yes, it is unfortunate when a four-year-old boy's mother is murdered. It's tragic and painful and bewildering."

"If you're here to give me a lecture about death and dying, Dr. Hamilton, I must tell you I find it offensive. My own daughter died just two years ago."

"Yes, I know and I'm terribly sorry for your loss," Keely said. On her feet now, she had no hope that Matthew would find a home here. And did she even want him to? He needed to be with a loving person, not someone whose capacity for mothering had died with her daughter.

And suddenly her impatience with Laura Barlow disappeared. Luke was right, she realized. This woman was not ready to make a long-term commitment to any child, particularly one with Matthew's turbulent past. Not only was it insensitive of Keely to try to push Laura like this, but it was unfair to Matthew. Blinded by her own urgent need to see the little boy settled, Keely had almost made a serious mistake in judgment.

She looked into the other woman's eyes with new understanding and spoke softly. "Nothing can ever fill that hole in your heart, can it?"

Tears sprang into Laura's eyes. "No. Nothing. Ever."

Keely drew a deep breath. "You know some-

thing? I just realized Luke was right when he tried
to tell me that if it was best for Matthew to be with
you, the way Phyllis wanted, you would welcome
the chance to take him. That I wouldn't have to
browbeat you into it. Which is what I've been doing. I'm sorry about that. It was a mistake for me
to come here again.''

"I'm sorry, too.'' Laura stood up. Although gracious, she was pale as she accompanied Keely to
the foyer. Her voice was slightly unsteady as she
spoke. "I wish I could give you the answer you
want, but as you point out, if it was meant to be,
I'd feel something in here—'' she touched her
chest "—wouldn't I?''

How could you not love Matthew? Keely wanted
to cry. But she held the words in. Instead, she
wished the woman happy holidays and left.

As she drove away, Keely tried to pinpoint what
it was about Laura that seemed different from the
first visit when Matthew and Luke had been with
her. Keely had felt some coolness, but the woman
wasn't the gushing type. Even after Laura realized
why they were there and had made plain her un-
willingness to take Matthew, Keely had not felt
unwelcome. But today there had been something
hostile in her manner. Why? And what had she
meant by her remark about Keely having inside
information about the way Randall felt about Matthew? She would have labeled it jealousy coming

from any other woman, but any suspicions along that line were so patently ridiculous, there had to be something else. Maybe Luke could explain it. She was his aunt.

All of which left them back at the beginning with Matthew. And today was typical of the problems they would encounter from here on out. Neither of them was free until eleven tonight when she would finally pick him up at Jenny Blackwell's house. As Keely neared the hospital, she faced the fact that with Phyllis gone, she would have to arrange for day care.

Two hours later, she was back in the E.R. and drawn immediately into an intense effort to save the life of a middle-aged biker, who had taken a nasty spill on the freeway when his Harley hit an ice patch. The first year intern who was working frantically trying to control bleeding from the biker's lacerated thigh looked up in obvious relief as Keely appeared. Chris Feldman had a promising career ahead of him, but his confidence was presently at rock bottom. He'd failed to diagnose a heart attack when a twenty-five-year-old pro basketball player had been admitted after ingesting cocaine and the athlete had died. The biker's condition was simpler, but just as urgent. Donning plastic gloves in case she needed to assist, Keely moved to Chris's side, watched in silence for a moment, then nodded in approval as the intern tied off the vein in the open wound. The eyes of everyone on the assisting team went to the overhead monitor and when the biker's vitals evened out, a collective murmur came from the team.

"Nice job, Chris," Keely said, stripping off her unused gloves.

"Thanks." With his sleeve, the intern wiped sweat from his brow, but he was clearly elated. "It was touch and go for a minute there. The EMT's almost lost him in the ambulance."

She patted his arm, smiling. "You did great."

She heard her name and glanced back to see Luke standing in the door. Her heart gave a little jump. If it hadn't been for Randall's phone call the night before, she and Luke would now be lovers. Phyllis's death had put a damper on their passion, but she knew it was only a matter of time until it happened again. The certainty sent a delicious sensation rippling through her.

"Can I see you a minute?" he asked.

"Sure. We'll be in the lounge if anybody asks," she told a nurse after tossing her gloves in the appropriate bin. Walking away with Luke, she said, "I was going to look you up as soon as I could grab a minute. I had to go out for a while."

"I know."

"You missed me?" But her smile faded at the look in his eyes. Uh-oh, he was ticked off about

something. She saw that the physician's lounge
was empty and went inside with him, heading for
a seat farthest from the door in case someone came
in. There were few places in the E.R. that were
private and if Luke's expression was any indication
of his mood, they would need privacy. She sat
down. Luke did not.

"When are you going to quit bugging Laura?"

She frowned. "How did you—"

"She called me an hour ago. She was upset. No,
more than that, she was depressed and crying. She
wanted to explain her reasons for refusing to do
what everybody seems to want to force on her."
He took a few steps in frustration before turning
back. "You've got to get off her back about Matthew!"

"Oh, God." Keely rubbed her forehead and
sighed with remorse. "I'm sorry," she said softly.

He stood looking as if he'd like to tell her exactly what she could do with her apology. "Don't
you get it yet? She's not the right person for Matthew."

"I know. I know."

"You know." He paused a moment. "Then why
in hell did you go over there this morning? And
why did you do it without consulting me? Aren't
we in this together?"

"We are." She gave a helpless gesture with
both hands while joyfully savoring the sound of

that "we." "But Phyllis's death changed things. You have to concede that. I felt she might agree if I gave it one more push, but now I—"

Luke let out an explosive breath. "What is it going to take to convince you, Keely? You're spinning your wheels with my aunt and uncle. We've got to look for other options for Matthew."

"I understand that now."

He drove all five fingers through his hair. "Then why—"

"It dawned on me while I was talking to her." She rose and moved to the window to gaze out pensively. "You've been right all along about this. Seeing their reluctance on that first visit, I should have accepted right then and there that they wouldn't be taking Matthew. I guess I was so focused on doing what Phyllis asked that I ignored everything else. She...Laura...is still grieving. It wouldn't be fair to Matthew even if she'd caved in and taken him simply because I kept pushing."

"He's doing fine with us for the time being," Luke said quietly.

She turned and saw that his anger was spent. "I guess that'll have to be enough until something better comes along, huh?" she stated with a small smile.

"Yeah, but we can't manage the way we've been doing."

"I know. After I left Laura, I went to check out

day care here at St. Dominic's. Chloe's been an angel to fill in when our schedules conflict—like today, for instance—but it'll be better for Matthew to have a regular schedule. He's starting there tomorrow morning."

"Good." Luke went to her, studying her with an expression in his eyes she couldn't read. Lifting a hand, he stroked the side of her cheek. "I'm sorry if I came on a little strong."

"It's okay." She turned her cheek into his warm palm, liking the feeling. "I was out of line."

"Yeah, you were." But his eyes were gentle now.

"I promise to keep you informed of any other wild ideas that come to me."

His smile came out fully then. "Uh-huh."

"And you'll do the same."

"I'm not usually given to wild impulses," he said, clearly teasing her.

"You could've fooled me."

She breathed in, held it, as his gaze moved to her lips. She could see in his eyes that they were both thinking of the night before.

A brisk knock pulled them back with a start. The door opened and Jenny Blackwell looked in. "Auto accident with three injured coming in," she said, adding as she backed out. "Two minutes ETA."

"Thanks, Jenny," Keely said, still looking into Luke's eyes.

"Hold that thought," he said.

Luke was elected to pick up Matthew from the Blackwell's house that night. Thirty minutes before their shift ended, Keely had admitted a patient in a diabetic coma, but she'd suddenly crashed. Then, after finally stabilizing the woman, her elderly husband had been so distraught he'd suffered severe chest pains, and Keely had had to stay to treat him. Only when she'd seen them both transferred upstairs to appropriate floors did she leave the hospital.

The trip home took only a few minutes on the deserted streets. A glance at her watch brought a groan as she pulled into the first available parking space. It was after midnight. Thinking of a warm shower and bed—and blanking out thoughts of Luke in it with her—she got out of her car. She needed to pick Matthew up at Luke's place, but first she had to let Oscar out for a bathroom run.

She had her key in her hand when she heard Oscar's frenzied barking. Quickly unlocking the door, she went inside. It was odd that he didn't rush to greet her, she thought, then realized he was closed up in the bathroom. Dropping her purse and keys on the foyer table, she headed down the hall, wondering if Luke had stopped in with Matthew and for some reason left Oscar confined. Strange, considering the lateness of the hour. But no, Luke didn't have a key to her apartment.

The instant she let him out, he bounded down the hall, still barking frantically, heading straight for the patio door in her bedroom. Clearly wanting out, he pawed and scratched at the door, ignoring Keely's command to be still. It was only as she held the straining dog that she realized the significance of finding the dog penned up in the bathroom.

"Easy, Oscar. It's okay, boy." Heart pounding, she went to her bedside table and turned on the lamp. When light flooded the room, she turned in a slow circle, checking for signs of an intruder. But everything seemed just as she'd left it.

There was no way Oscar could have shut himself up in the bathroom. Someone had been inside her house. Again. She sank onto the bed and called Oscar over to see if he was hurt, but he seemed fine. She released him and again he went straight to the patio door, nosing at the carpet, whining and scratching to get out.

Moving closer, Keely saw something shiny on the floor, just visible beneath the folds of the drapes. Lipstick. Or rather the case from one of her lipsticks. Then she noticed a streak of color on the drapes. Holding her breath, she slowly pulled the cord to draw the drapes. This time, he'd left a message scrawled on the glass in crude letters: *"I WANT MY KID, BITCH!"*

CHAPTER EIGHT

DETECTIVE JAMES EVANS WAS a huge black man with penetrating green eyes and an abundance of curly salt-and-pepper hair. In spite of the cold night, he wore no coat, only a down vest over a dress shirt and a tie printed with tumbling Santas. He had arrived soon after the two policemen who had answered the 9-1-1 call placed by Luke. Shocked and terrified after reading the obscene threat written on the patio door, Keely had had only one thought—to get out of the apartment. She had run straight to Luke.

She shuddered now, feeling violated and angry and confused. "I can't believe this has happened," she murmured.

Bending, he examined the catch on her front door. "You say there's nothing missing?"

"I don't think so." Keely perched gingerly on the edge of the couch with Oscar at her feet. "I think he just wanted to scare me with that message."

Evans studied the big dog. "Any idea how he managed to shut your dog up in the bathroom?"

"Not really," Keely said, rubbing Oscar's ears. "Usually he's leery around strangers. It's unthinkable he would have let someone just walk in."

"Some criminals have a winning way with animals."

Luke, who had been fuming and pacing, stopped to look at Keely. "When you realized that Oscar was penned up in the bathroom, you shouldn't have gone inside."

Keely released an impatient huff. "I didn't *know* he was penned up until I got inside, Luke. Then when he came out of the bathroom heading for the patio door, I really wasn't thinking. I guess I was just carried along in the excitement of the moment."

"There would have been real excitement if Billy Long had been waiting for you in the bedroom," Luke growled.

"Who's Billy Long?" Evans asked.

"The jerk who did this," Luke snapped.

"The jerk we *think* did this," Keely replied.

"Did you change the locks like I told you to?" Luke demanded.

"I meant to," she said, ignoring his scowl. "I just never got around to it. I know, I know…I'll do it first thing in the morning."

Evans flipped to a new page in his notebook. "I'd take his advice if I were you, Dr. Hamilton. It isn't easy for us to do anything about stalking.

First of all, we don't have the manpower to keep an eye on you twenty-four hours a day, so if a guy is looking to scare a woman, all he has to do is watch her habits and choose his moment. I don't want to alarm you unnecessarily, but you can do a lot to protect yourself by taking a few precautions.''

"Am I being stalked?" Keely asked. Her hands, stroking Oscar, went still.

Luke made an explosive sound. "What the hell would you call the message on your door? Damn right, you're being stalked."

Evans consulted his notes. "Any idea why this…Billy Long has it in for you, Dr. Hamilton? Is he a patient? Someone who admires you?"

"She has his son," Luke said.

"You're married to the guy?" Evans asked with surprise.

"No!" She gave Luke an exasperated look. "That's not what he meant."

Luke sat down heavily beside Keely on the couch. "The boy's mother was murdered a few days ago. We think Billy did it. When Phyllis left him, she asked Keely to look after Matthew. It seems plain that Billy wants Matthew."

"Why?" After scribbling a few words, Evans looked up. "If he killed the mother, why would he care about the kid? Seems to me a four-year-old would be a burden he doesn't need."

"Who knows!" Luke said irritably. "That's for the psychologists to figure out."

"He's not even Matthew's father," Keely said, spreading her hands in bewilderment. "You've got a point, Detective Evans, why would he want Matthew?"

"Who is the kid's father?" Evans asked, pen poised above his notebook.

Keely shrugged. "Nobody knows. Phyllis's personal effects held precious little information, and on Matthew's birth certificate it said the father was deceased."

"I'll nose around," Evans said, closing his notebook. "See what I can find out. In the meantime, I'd be real careful, Dr. Hamilton. Change those locks, as your friend suggests. If it is this Billy Long, the message he left could be just an attempt to harass you because he thinks you may have influenced his wife to leave him. He might have no intention of saddling himself with the kid, but since we don't know that, I wouldn't take any chances with the boy if I were you." He tucked the notebook in an inside pocket in the vest. "Where's Matthew right now?"

"Asleep in the guest bedroom," Keely said. Luke had carried him over, still sleeping, after the cops arrived.

Luke was on his feet now. "And I'll be staying tonight."

Keely looked at him. "It's late, Luke. You have to be at the hospital at seven tomorrow. You don't have to—"

"It's already done. Chris Feldman's filling in for me. He sends his regards."

"Oh."

A technician appeared from the bedroom carrying a black case. "We're done here, Detective. We dusted for prints in the bathroom and at the glass door and got nothing. It looks like the lady's visitor was real careful, or he wiped the place clean before he left."

"Great," Luke muttered. "Nothing to prove he was here even if Atlanta P.D. does manage to find him."

"I'll be happy to forget that he broke into my house if they can just take him out of circulation," Keely said, rubbing her arms briskly. She was still trying to cope with the thought that she was being stalked. She was no celebrity and she wasn't in a sick relationship. Worse, she couldn't help thinking how much that message scrawled on her door looked more like blood than lipstick.

"Dr. Jamison has a point," Detective Evans said. "Unless we manage to connect Long to his wife's murder or this incident, even if we do find him we may not be able to hold him."

"He killed Phyllis!" Keely said with outrage,

looking at both men. "Surely you won't let him go."

Beside her, Luke shoved balled fists into his pockets. "Just find him, Detective," he told Evans, his silver eyes hard. "Then worry about how to hold him."

TEN MINUTES LATER Luke and Keely watched the activity in the parking lot as Detective Evans's team packed up to leave. Then, as the policemen pulled out, a dark Lexus wheeled into the vacant space nearest her front door. Luke, standing beside Keely, muttered a soft oath. "Now what? It's the middle of the night, for Christ's sake."

Keely, however, instantly recognized the man getting out of the big car. "It's Randall," she said in surprise.

"So it is," Luke replied dryly. He waited as his uncle headed toward them, then placed an arm around Keely's waist. "He probably heard about your latest escapade."

Startled as much by his touch as what he said, Keely turned and looked at him. "You make it sound as if this is about me, and it isn't. Billy just wants Matthew."

"It's possible," he said. "But Matthew's with me half the time and I don't see anybody breaking into my place."

Something in his look stole her breath. "Maybe he doesn't know you're involved."

"Or maybe he blames you for everything that's happened," Luke said flatly. Then he caught her chin and gave her a quick, hard kiss just as Randall Barlow mounted the steps. "And it's high time we let him know you're not like Phyllis, a woman without protection."

"Uh, am I interrupting?"

"Dr. Barlow." Flustered, Keely managed a smile and tried to step back to let him inside, but instead she came up against Luke's hard thighs.

"I know it's late, but I was in the hospital with a former parishioner who had a heart attack tonight, and then someone said there had been another break-in here."

"Yeah, you missed all the excitement," Luke said, leaning around her to shake his uncle's hand.

"Are you all right?" Randall asked, giving Keely a concerned look. "I thought of Billy Long right away. What's it going to take to stop him?"

"I'm fine, Dr. Barlow."

"Please, it's Randall." He looked at Luke. "What do you suggest to keep Keely and the boy safe, Luke? This is an area where you have some experience. We can't just wait until he strikes before doing something, can we?"

"I'm staying with her tonight," Luke said, his

hand tightening possessively on her waist. "There was no need for you to drive over here."

Luke, too? Randall seemed to miss the undercurrent in Luke's voice, but Keely heard it, the same ridiculous suspicion she'd picked up in Laura Barlow's manner earlier.

"Actually, I was going to suggest that Keely and the boy spend the night at my home. I don't like the idea of her being alone while that maniac is stalking her." He looked at Keely. "Have you called your mother?"

"My mother?" she echoed faintly.

"She should be told what's going on. I know, if you were my daughter, I wouldn't want you to handle this on your own. This is a time for the support and protection of your family."

"I'm not family," Luke said with an edge in his voice, "but she's not without support. I'm going to be here until morning, when we'll all head for the hospital. Matthew's in day care now." He paused, giving his uncle a steely-eyed look. "Unless you're suggesting that Laura has had a change of heart."

"No, no, she—" Randall paused, then rubbed gently at a spot near his temple as if he felt a headache coming on. "Unfortunately, she's unwilling to make a permanent commitment as far as Matthew's concerned, but this threat to Keely puts everything in a different light."

"To you maybe. But not necessarily to Laura." Luke's arm was still firmly about Keely's waist. "As I said, I'm staying with Keely and Matthew tonight. And I'll see to it that they're safe tomorrow."

Luke watched as Keely closed the door after Randall left. "He wanted me to call my mother," she said with an ironic look.

"He's concerned about you," Luke said. "Too concerned."

"You're way off track there," she told him, moving toward the living room. "Randall Barlow isn't interested in me that way."

"Oh? Well, you sure as hell could have fooled me."

"He's a nice man, an ordained minister, for heaven's sake. And we're friends. Besides, he understands my sense of responsibility about Matthew because he shares it. Phyllis managed to touch us both that night at the hospital, and then she was killed. In a sense we both feel she left in our hands the care of her little boy and neither one of us is going to be able to walk away until Matthew's future is settled."

"I can't see that Randall's doing a hell of a lot. Talk's cheap. In my view, there's no risk to Randall in simply offering moral support. *You're* the one whose life is turned upside down trying to provide for Matthew."

"*We're* providing for him," she reminded him with a wry smile. "You and me, Luke. Matthew's turned your life upside down, too."

"Yeah. And I'm still trying to figure out how it happened."

She touched his arm. "It happened because you're a very nice man."

He grunted something between oh-yeah and aw-shucks, making Keely smile. But then, as she headed across to the Christmas tree, her expression changed. "You can't understand the irony in all this, Luke," she said, touching a small nativity scene enclosed in a glass ornament.

"What's ironic about it?"

"Randall Barlow is urging me to call my mother."

Luke was confused. "What's odd about that? Fact is, it was the one thing he said that I agreed with. You might want to consider staying a while with your mother, just until they find Long."

"I don't think so. But I'll be careful until he's apprehended. I won't take any chances."

"Well, at least you're admitting this is dangerous."

"This is my oldest ornament," Keely said softly, making it swing gently with a touch of her finger. "I got it when I was about six. My mother was working two jobs, one at a department store.

See, it has a hairline crack right here. It was damaged, so she was able to afford it.''

Luke guessed from her expression that this was about something more than a Christmas ornament. He moved closer.

''It's Mary, Joseph and the baby Jesus. I used to pretend I had a family like that, just me, my mom and my dad.'' She laughed softly. ''Only thing was, I didn't have a dad, never had. Not only was he not around, I didn't even know his name.''

''Tough,'' Luke murmured. His father had been a strict son of a bitch, but he'd at least been there.

''Yeah. My mother got pregnant when she was sixteen and the boy who impregnated her gave her three hundred dollars to get an abortion, but she didn't do it. Instead, she left New Orleans without telling him.''

Luke listened, realizing he was intensely interested in the twist of fate that had molded Keely into the determined, fiercely independent woman she'd become. ''So some lucky man has a fabulous daughter, but he doesn't know it?''

A fleeting smile crossed her face. ''As far as I know, no. So I never expected him to show up one day and say, 'Daddy's home.'''

And the longing in her heart for that moment when her daddy would claim her and love her was still there, Luke thought, wanting to put his arms around her. ''You never knew who he was?''

Keely paused to adjust some of the lights on the tree. "Well, I didn't for years and years, but as I grew older, the need to know became almost an obsession. I constantly pestered my mother to answer my questions. She didn't want to, knowing the repercussions might be unpleasant. So for a long time, the issue caused a lot of trouble between us. In fact, I think now that a major part of my rebellion when I ran away was my need to find that other half of my identity." She looked back at him over her shoulder. "Having always had both your parents, you might not be able to understand that."

"It sounds pretty natural," Luke said.

"Mom finally told me everything after we were reunited in New Orleans. She'd just married Daniel and they were so happy that I think she wanted to do everything she could to make me happy, even if naming him opened a can of worms."

"What happened then? Did you look him up?"

"In a way. I found him, but I didn't tell him who I was." She laughed uneasily, staring at her hands. "I mean, you can't walk up to a man and say, guess what, I'm your long-lost daughter, the one you never knew you had."

She was pale. With a muttered oath, Luke gave up the effort to keep his distance. He slipped his arms around her from behind, pulling her close and resting his chin on the top of her head. "So you know who he is, but he still doesn't know about you?'' He felt the sigh that went through her as she yielded to his embrace.

"That's about the size of it, I guess."

"Who is it, Keely?"

She shook her head sadly. "Would you believe? It's Randall Barlow."

CHAPTER NINE

WHAT WAS SHE DOING? What had she *done!* Keely turned over restlessly, drove a fist into her pillow, then flopped onto her back, staring once again at the ceiling. She hadn't even told her *mother* that she'd looked up Randall Barlow, that he was in Atlanta. That she'd chosen St. Dominic's Hospital for her residency because he was chaplain there. That her longing just to know her father had pushed her to such ridiculous extremes that if she couldn't be his daughter, then she was willing to settle for a professional association.

When she'd first arrived, it had been enough just to work with him, to see him daily, to consult with him on cases such as Phyllis Long's, to seek him out to ease the moments when she was forced to tell families bad news. The more she worked with Randall Barlow, the more she came to admire him. She'd been thrilled that her father was everything she'd secretly dreamed he'd be. Time had passed. Then more time. And then his daughter had died. The moment when she might have felt right in approaching him with such a stunning revelation was lost, and she'd never quite found the right time to tell him since.

So why had she told Luke?

Was her impulsive confession a sort of backdoor method of revealing who she was? Keely groaned and turned over again, burying her face in her pillow. If so, it was just too pathetic. Besides, she couldn't see Luke taking it upon himself to tell her secret. He was a man who would honor a confidence, not blab it without regard for its significance to his own aunt and uncle.

No, she should have enough courage to tell Randall face-to-face, not manipulate a situation to escape the possibly unpleasant repercussions once Randall and Laura knew. Laura, oh Lord. Keely was not one of Laura Barlow's favorite people. Only God knew how she would react when she found out that Keely was Randall's illegitimate daughter.

Plus, there were other complications. Thanks to Phyllis Long and Matthew, she and her father were both tangled in a web of circumstances that would have to be resolved and Keely worried that Laura seemed to have a problem with that, too.

Smothering another moan, she turned over once again, yanking at her gown, now twisted into a pretzel around her. She considered turning on the light and simply giving up all pretense at sleeping. On top of everything else, she was intensely aware of Luke on the couch in her living room. And until she got the locks changed on her doors, she could tell by the stubborn set of his jaw when he'd demanded a pillow and an extra blanket that he was going to insist on practically moving in.

She wasn't sure how she felt about his being around that much. A shiver rippled through her as she recalled how close she'd come to losing her head the other night. If it hadn't been for that phone call from Randall telling them about Phyllis's death, there would have been no turning back.

At a small sound in the hall, she came up on one elbow. Was Matthew awake? A shadow moved at her door, then materialized into Luke's tall, broad shape.

"Is it Matthew?" she asked.

"He's okay."

She could see in the moonlight from her window that he wore dark boxers and nothing else. She reached for the lamp on her bedside table, then changed her mind.

"Having trouble sleeping?" he asked.

"I have a lot on my mind," she said, scrambling into a sitting position. He seemed totally unaware of being almost naked.

"Yeah. Me, too." A second passed, then he headed for her bed. "Scoot over."

"What?"

"It's chilly," he said as if that was reason

enough to climb into her bed. And before she had a chance to decide whether to allow it or not, he was there, plumping up the pillows, pushing them against the headboard and pulling her into the curve of his arm as he leaned back, releasing a deep breath. "I heard you in here tossing and turning. We might as well keep each other company."

She could send him away with one word, Keely thought, giving it about five seconds before rejecting that idea. It felt...right somehow snuggled against him this way. He was big and warm and he smelled like the soap in her shower and healthy male.

"No arguments?" he asked. She felt him angle his chin a little so he could look at her.

"I'm too tired to argue."

"Whoa. That's gotta be a first."

She sensed he was smiling and poked him with an elbow. "Be polite or you're back on the couch." After a moment, she said, "I think you should forget what I told you."

"You sure know how to drop a bombshell, I'll say that."

"I don't know why I—I mean, considering your connection to Randall and Laura, it was totally inappropriate."

He shrugged noncommittally. She moved to look up at him. "You won't say anything?"

He touched her mouth with one finger. "It's your secret, Keely."

"Thanks." On impulse, she kissed his fingertip and heard the quick intake of his breath. But before he could react, she shifted and again lay in the circle of his arm. She was acutely aware of his broad chest, the strength of his arm about her, hard as iron. Her heart was beating fast. Any man would interpret that as an invitation. Maybe it was. "What're we doing, Luke?"

The steady sound of his breathing stopped, then resumed. "Nothing...yet."

"I don't think it's smart to start anything," she said huskily, but her arm tingled where his warm palm glided slowly up and down her skin. Imagining how it would feel to have his hands elsewhere—everywhere!—sent a burst of heat through her.

"We've already started something, Keely." He turned suddenly and pulled her down until they lay facing each other. She gave a tiny gulp when he pushed his thigh between her legs. "Tonight we get to the good part."

The room was dark, but she could see the outline of his features. Luke's face had always appealed to her. And since they'd been thrown together for Matthew's sake, she'd come to like other things about him, things more important than how he looked. It was more than mere approval she felt now, but there was still a scrap of rebellion in her. In their present relationship, he was demanding and overprotective. What would he be like as a lover? "I haven't decided if I want us to get involved that way," she told him.

Now his hand was cupping her chin as he considered what she said. "But you've been thinking about it?"

"Well…" She did all she could not to shiver as his thumb skimmed slowly over her lips. If he was going to kiss her, she wished he'd go ahead and do it. If? Of course he was going to kiss her. He probably planned to do a lot more than kissing.

"While you're trying to decide," he said, gathering her even closer so that now they were touching from chest to toe, "maybe this'll help." He dipped his head and brushed her mouth with his. Just that one quick taste sent her heart fluttering wildly. What was it about this man?

As he nuzzled the softness beneath her chin, he was smiling. She knew it because…she just knew it. She gave a little sigh and arched her neck. And then he was sliding his tongue over her skin in a trail all the way down to the vee of her nightgown. This time there was no controlling the tremor that rippled through her.

There was very little light, but Luke watched her face as he stroked her nipples through the silky gown. He'd been so wild for her that night on the couch that he'd wasted the opportunity to savor her. He'd waste no opportunities tonight.

"Luke..." His name ended on a moan as he suckled deeply while his hands caressed flesh he'd fantasized about since the moment she'd first issued a curt order in the E.R., looking at him with those sexy amber eyes as if he was no different than a dozen other residents she commanded.

She put out a hand to touch him, caressing his chest, moving her palm over his hot skin, tangling her fingers in the crinkly hair. "Now, Luke..."

The look of her nearly sent him over the edge. For months he'd wanted to be the one to demolish Keely's self-control, to turn her into the wanton lover of his fantasies. What he hadn't expected was to be pushed beyond the limits of his own control.

His hands were shaky as he caught her face and waited until she opened her eyes. "Have you decided, Keely?"

"What?" She stared at him.

"You know where we're headed."

"I want you," she said, her voice low and thick. "But I'm not...I don't have—"

"It's okay. I have something." He kissed her once deeply, then murmuring words, endearments, scraps of thoughts that would later make him shake his head in bafflement, he pulled her gown off and tossed it aside. As eager as he, her hands were already working at his boxers. He helped her strip them away, freeing him, fully, painfully aroused.

Keely touched him gently and he groaned his approval. He wanted nothing more now than to be buried deep inside her, craving the sensation that would come when he would finally make her his. He reached for the tiny foil square lying on the bedside table.

Once he was ready, he bent and kissed her face, her throat, her ear while his hand sought out warmer, more intimate places. "Tell me you want me."

"I do, I do."

Then, with fingers only, he sent her hurtling over the edge. Luke held her while the storm raged, savoring a fierce satisfaction as she was caught in wave after wave of wild pleasure.

Lowering her back to the bed, he paused. "Are you ready for me, sweetheart?"

Boneless and temporarily sated, she smiled at him. "Yes." She stretched like a cat, an amber-eyed, contented cat. He almost lost it then. In response, he gripped her hips and in one strong thrust buried himself inside her.

Keely gasped, her head reeling at the power and strength of his possession. Pleasure shot through her as each stroke seemed to go deeper and deeper until her body was a mass of unfocused sensation. And then she felt the onslaught of another orgasm.

As it erupted, she could do no more than hold on, to wrap herself around him and let him take her with him, wherever and however he chose.

When he buried his face in her hair for his own explosive climax, it seemed the most natural thing in the world to tell him.

"I love you," she said.

"RANDALL, IT'S SO LATE. When are you coming to bed?"

Randall returned a photograph to the file and removed his reading glasses. With his thumb and forefinger, he massaged his eyes. It was late. And he wasn't getting anywhere plowing through these files. His wife left the doorway and came forward with a curious look, frowning at the jumble of paper littering his desk.

"What are you working on?" Catching sight of one picture, she gasped. "Randall! Is that a dead body?"

He quickly gathered the photos and slipped them into an envelope. "Detective Evans allowed me to look through Phyllis Long's file. These pictures were taken at the crime scene."

Laura's hand covered her mouth. "They're horrible! I don't know how you can bear to look at such gruesome things."

He curbed a sharp reply and spoke quietly. "I

know you don't understand, Laura, but I still feel some responsibility in all this.''

"Responsibility?'' She stared, clearly mystified. "What on earth do you mean? You had nothing to do with that woman's death.''

"No, of course not. That isn't what I meant.''

"What then? It's tragic that she died, but you've had other parishioners, other patients at the hospital who've died and you haven't felt any moral obligation. And you've never once been tempted to get involved in any criminal investigation! What can you do, for heaven's sake?''

"I don't know. I just thought someone looking at it with a fresh eye might see something Evans or his men had missed.'' He shrugged. "I know it's a long shot, but—''

"A long shot.'' He might have been speaking a foreign language, she looked so baffled. "I can't understand what has come over you, Randall.''

He met her eyes. "Can't you?''

Her tone changed. "It's the little boy, isn't it?'' she asked with a beseeching look, as if she wanted to hear him deny it.

"Yes, it's Matthew. Of course, it's Matthew.'' Randall leaned back with a sigh, again rubbing his eyes. "And Keely, too.''

She turned away abruptly. "Keely,'' she said coolly.

He was silent for a heartbeat. "Laura what has Keely done to make you so disapproving?"

"I just don't understand your...your obsession with her!"

"I—" He stopped, shaking his head. He was not obsessed with Keely, but he did feel a connection that somehow seemed to go beyond their mutual concern for Matthew. But how could he explain it to his wife when he couldn't explain it to himself? "Go back to bed, Laura." He started to open the file folder in front of him. "I'm going to be here a while."

"Just tell me what you're looking for."

Frowning, he picked up the initial report made by a rookie cop, who'd been first on the scene. "I don't know. Something. Anything that might help us find Billy Long."

"And thus remove the threat to Keely."

Lifting his gaze, he looked at her. "Under the circumstances, if anything happens to Keely, Matthew is truly in trouble."

"Naturally we're back to that."

"This has always been about Matthew."

"A fact I'm reminded of daily," she said bitterly. Moving away, she wrapped her arms around herself and began pacing. "I'm never allowed to forget it. I'm constantly badgered to reconsider and made to feel mean and petty because I have perfectly natural misgivings about taking in a four-year-old child.'' She turned, an imploring expression on her face. ''You, of all people should understand. One child can't replace another. Matthew isn't Shelley. Is my attitude so selfish? Is my grief for my daughter just pathetic self-pity?''

He stood up but did not go to her. ''No one's suggesting that Matthew will replace Shelley. But if you would give him a chance, you might find that having him would be a welcome distraction.'' He paused, wondering if he could make her see his point. ''You live each day with sadness and grief. If Matthew was around, you would be—''

''I would be what, Randall? I would be running and fetching and answering endless questions, wiping his nose, washing his hands. Saying do this, Matthew, do that, Matthew!'' Losing her composure, tears were glistening now and her tone was rising. ''Well, it won't work! Don't you see that? I've done all that for my little girl and she's gone. I don't even want to *think* about doing it for any other child. Matthew and his fate is your crusade— yours and your precious Keely's. So the two of you—'' she struggled to regain control, then added in a hard tone ''—and Luke, since she seems to have captivated him, too—can work this out among yourselves. J-just leave m-me out of it!''

''Laura—'' He started toward her, but stopped when she put out a hand.

''No, I'm going to bed. I don't want to talk

about this anymore.'' She lifted her chin even though it was unsteady. ''Are you coming or not?''

He glanced down at the material strewn across his desk, then back up into her eyes. ''Not yet,'' he said quietly.

An expression of pain settled on her face. ''Well, then…'' She started to leave, but hesitated when he called her name.

''It was never my intent—or anyone else's—to make you feel unworthy concerning your feelings about taking Matthew. Feelings are…just what they are. We can't dictate them and sometimes we can't control them.'' His gaze went to a photo of Phyllis Long. ''It'll all work out, Laura. The police will find Billy, the threat to Keely and Matthew will be gone and somebody—a mom and dad— will turn up who need a little boy as much as he needs them.''

She stood a moment, simply staring at him. Then using her fingers, she wiped moisture from both her cheeks. With a look she indicated the paper on his desk. At the cost of some measure of her pride, she asked, ''Are you certain this can't wait until morning?''

''I'm into it right now,'' he said. ''It makes sense to stick with it.'' Their talk had changed nothing, he thought, while the gulf between them was widening. ''Don't worry, I'll sleep in the guest room so I don't disturb you when I'm finished here.''

"I'LL SLEEP IN THE GUEST ROOM."

In all the years of their marriage, there had never been a night when Randall had slept apart from her. They'd quarreled, of course, but they'd always observed that wise adage about never going to sleep in anger. She turned to the framed photo on her bedside table and looked into the beautiful eyes of their daughter. Shelley at sixteen, radiant and smiling. So much promise, such vitality. *So alive!*

A wave of anguish rose in her. Her throat tightened, but the tears came anyway. There had been disapproval in the eyes of her husband. And disappointment. Feelings just were, he'd said. And those were his. He was aligned with Keely and Luke, not her! It was an alien thought and she was so shaken by it that she was gripped by a chilling and frightening possibility.

Her daughter was gone. Was she losing her husband, too?

CHAPTER TEN

WELL, NOW SHE KNEW. Keely stood at her cabinet looking at breakfast foods without really seeing anything. She'd wondered what kind of lover Luke would be and he was…well, words failed her. Almost. He was considerate, creative, sometimes tender, sometimes wild. She might have some doubt about his sensitivity in dealing with patients, but as a lover he was fantastic. After last night, she was aching in places that made her blush.

Matthew tugged at her sleep shirt. "I'm hungry, Keely."

She looked down into his little face. "I'm sorry, honey bun. I was daydreaming."

"Your eyes were open."

"And now I'm wide-awake." She gave him a quick hug and, after boosting him up on a chair, reached for a box of instant oatmeal. "What'll it be this morning, kiddo? Cinnamon-raisin, maple or apple-nut oatmeal?"

"I'm waiting to see what Luke wants."

As she reached for a plastic carton to pour him some milk, she heard the shower stop. Instantly a mental image of Luke, naked and wet, materialized. Did he towel off and put on those silky boxers and then shave, or did he stand at the sink, sans boxers, extravagantly male, to use his razor?

"I bet Luke likes Froot Loops."

She blinked the fantasy away and looked at Matthew. "What, sweetie?"

The little boy reached for his milk. "Me and Luke like the same stuff and I bet he won't choose *oatmeal.*"

"We'll see," she said, opening the box of instant cereal. "How 'bout cinnamon-raisin?"

"Hey! How's it goin', champ?" Luke breezed in smelling of aftershave and warm, still-damp male. Grabbing a piece of toast, he gave Matthew's sandy curls a quick ruffle, tossed Oscar a piece of crust and shot Keely a sexy smile before he crunched into the toast. He radiated male vitality and good humor. In a denim shirt and tan chinos, he looked just as good as he smelled.

She was uncertain about morning-after protocol, but shouldn't he be just a tad less...cocksure? Oh Lord, she didn't believe she'd even thought that! Besides, she'd been as willing as he to allow their relationship to move to an intimate level. She'd known for some time that her feelings for Luke were different from anything she'd ever felt for another man, but she hadn't been prepared for the sheer power of her response. There'd been an urgency and a need in him that had tapped into something equally urgent and compelling in her. It almost seemed as if she'd entered another universe. Studying him from beneath her lashes, she wondered if he'd felt anything like that. They had not talked much last night.

"Are you really gonna eat oatmeal, Luke?" Matthew asked, wrinkling his nose.

"Whoa! I never—" Luke stopped short when Keely kicked his ankle. She was holding the envelope of instant oatmeal and sending a distinct message with her eyes. "Uh, I never get enough of—" he studied the label "—cinnamon-raisin oatmeal."

"Well, I like Froot Loops better," Matthew said, looking glum.

"Hey, Froot Loops are for *little* kids. This stuff'll put iron in your pipes and hair on your chest, buddy-boy."

"But I don't have any pipes," Matthew said. "And nobody I play with has hair on their chest."

"Just kidding," Luke told him, then winked at Keely. "Peer pressure, it's already started."

Straddling a chair, he watched Keely dump two portions of the dehydrated cereal into bowls, one for each of them. Sticking them under the faucet, she mixed water into the flakes and then popped both into the microwave. "Where's yours?" he asked.

"Oh, I'll grab something later," she said, plunking the warm gray gunk down in front of them. "*Bon appétit,* guys," she said, darting a wicked grin at Luke. But he was too quick when she tried to zip past him. He caught her around the waist and his hand snaked beneath her short sleep shirt. After last night, the look in his eye combined with the feel of his warm palm gliding up her soft inner thigh was enough to stop her in her tracks.

"Something bugging you, lady?"

"I need to get dressed," she breathed, trying to ignore the delicious sensations curling through her.

"Are you hurting, Keely?" Matthew asked, watching anxiously. Instant understanding flashed in both Keely's and Luke's eyes. Beside them, Oscar gave a happy woof, wagging his tail.

"Nah," Luke said, releasing her and giving the boy a reassuring squeeze on his shoulder. "See, Oscar knows I'm just teasing."

"Luke would never hurt me, Matthew," Keely said, putting a kiss on the end of the boy's nose with her forefinger.

Matthew studied them both for a moment, then relaxed.

"All right."

"Okay, guys, eat up." Keely forced an authoritative tone in her voice. "We need to be out of here in twenty minutes."

KEELY HAD BEEN LOOKING forward to leaving work on time that day since, for once, she and Luke were on the same schedule. Then ten minutes before she could escape, a suicidal college student was admitted. He'd been coaxed down from a ledge outside the window of his seventh-floor dorm room by a seasoned cop and transported to the hospital. Keely was trying to calm him when the admissions clerk hurried into the treatment cubicle.

"Dr. Hamilton, you're wanted at the nurses station," she said.

"In a moment, Wendy." Without looking at the clerk, she took a scrap of paper from the distraught student. "I'm going to call your parents, Jacob. Since they're in Florida, it'll take a while for them to get here. Until they do, we'll admit you and someone will be in to talk to you about this."

"They'll kill me."

"Our counselors don't kill patients, Jacob," she said dryly.

"I mean my parents. They'll kill me when they find out."

"So you were going to jump out of that window to keep them from killing you?" She smiled gently and squeezed his hand. "Isn't there something wrong with that plan?"

"You don't know them," he said glumly.

"Flunking out isn't the end of the world. You'll have next semester to make up those grades."

"My dad's a Phi Beta Kappa and my mom belongs to Mensa. They'll never understand."

"They love you, don't they?"

He shrugged. "I guess."

She patted his hand. "Well, then…"

"Dr. Hamilton?" The clerk met her eyes anxiously.

"In a minute, Wendy."

"The day-care center called. It's about Matthew."

"Matthew?" Keely's fear was a knife stab all the way to her heart. My God, had Billy Long managed to get to Matthew in the day-care center? "Has he been kidnapped?"

"No, there's been an accident."

Now her heart completely stopped. The image of Matthew battered and broken flashed into her mind. "Is it? What…what happened?"

"I'm sorry, Dr. Hamilton. I didn't talk to them. Dr. Jamison did."

"Luke?" She put a hand on her throat.

"He asked me to find you and tell you not to rush over there. He'll call you and give you a report.

A report. No, she wanted to see Matthew for herself. She was almost out of the room before remembering her patient. Forcing herself to calm down, she went back to him. "Jacob, Wendy will stay with you until someone comes to take you upstairs.''

''It's okay. I'll be all right. I'm sorry about your little boy. I hope he's not hurt too bad.''

Murmuring something, she headed for the nearest exit. Driving would be quickest, she thought, punching the elevator button to take her to the garage. The day-care center was on the hospital grounds, but it was all the way on the other side, set apart in a separate building. She danced impatiently, waiting for the elevator, and when it pinged and slid open, she lurched into it, almost colliding with Randall.

''Matthew's hurt!'' she blurted out, the panic inside her weakening her knees.

''Is it Billy Long?'' he asked instantly, placing an arm around her shoulders.

''No. At least, I don't think so. Wendy just said he'd had an accident.'' Shaking her head, wanting—needing—to turn into his embrace, she sucked in a calming breath. Next to Luke, only Randall truly understood her emotions where Matthew was concerned. But she would be no good to Matthew in a state of panic. ''I need to get over there.''

''To day care?''

''Yes! Right now.''

''Does Luke know?''

''Wendy said he's there now.'' She pressed her

lips together to stop them trembling. "I don't care if he is, I want to see Matthew with my own eyes." She looked up into Randall's brown eyes. "I was going to my car."

"Alone? To the parking garage?" His hand still rubbed her shoulders reassuringly. "Do you think that's wise? Whoever's stalking you could be watching. I bet Luke would want you to wait until he can give you a progress report."

"I don't care what he wants! And I'm tired of this…this lowlife who's too cowardly to show himself." She felt herself losing it again. "I want to see Matthew!"

"Then I'll go with you." His arm tightened around her in a reassuring hug. "But first let's stop at my office and call over there." When she opened her mouth to object, he added, "What if you miss them because they're on their way to the E.R.? It'll just take a minute."

Turning, he touched her waist to urge her toward his office, fortunately just around the corner and a few doors down. He was right, of course, but Keely was a person who liked action. She needed to *do* something in a crisis. Calmly calling to find out about Matthew was not the way she did things.

"Here we are," Randall said, finding the right card in his Rolodex in seconds. Before she could lunge for the telephone, he had dialed the number. "Randall Barlow here, Mrs. Wilson. We're concerned about Matthew Long. He is? Dr. Jamison, eh? Well, that's a relief, I can tell you. Dr. Hamilton was…well, frantic. Yes, yes. Thank you, Mrs. Wilson.''

''What is it? What's going on? Is he okay?'' Keely's questions tumbled over themselves in her panic.

''He's fine. Luke's bringing him here so you can see for yourself.'' He replaced the receiver. ''He had an accident on the monkey bars when another little boy tried to help him up to the highest level. He pulled Matthew's arm out of its socket. And nobody on the staff felt competent enough to pop it back into place in spite of the fact that it must have been hurting him terribly. Luke took one look, slipped it back into place and he's right as rain as we speak.'' He gave her a big smile.

But Keely wasn't able to smile. Her face crumpled and the tears she'd controlled since hearing Matthew was hurt welled up and ran over.

Seeing her expression, Randall again put his arm about her and this time, she turned her face into his shoulder and let the tears flow. It was such a blessed relief to know he was all right. That Billy Long hadn't managed to get to him. That he wouldn't be a casualty in the E.R. Not Matthew. She saw too much of that.

''Now, now, Keely, aren't you letting your

imagination run away with you?'' He was patting her sympathetically.

"I...I'm just so…''

"Working in E.R. does tend to make us fear the worst, doesn't it?'' he observed in a dry tone. Reaching behind her, he plucked a couple of tissues from a box and offered them to her. Keely was almost amused. He must do this a lot; he was so good at it. Just as she started to move away, someone knocked but didn't wait to enter. Both turned to see Laura Barlow framed in the doorway of her husband's office.

For a frozen heartbeat, nobody spoke. Laura's eyes were wide with shock. Keely realized how it must look, her clinging to Randall, teary eyed, the moment obviously emotional. Her mind went blank searching for a simple explanation for what, to Randall's wife, was clearly suspect. He released Keely, but he made no move to go to his wife. Her heart sinking, Keely took a step back, but she knew she was blushing. Looking guilty!

"I didn't expect you, Laura,'' Randall said, giving her a puzzled smile. "Did I forget a date?''

"I thought I'd surprise you,'' Laura said in a shaken tone. And then she gathered herself and spoke coldly. "I can see I chose the wrong time to visit.''

"Nonsense,'' Randall said. "Keely and I were just—''

"Please, Randall," Laura said. "I've had my suspicions long enough. I can hardly deny the evidence of my own eyes. I've never believed what people say, that the workplace teems with…with relationships between—"

"Mrs. Barlow—" Keely stepped forward.

"Don't!" Laura raised her hand and cut her off. "This is between my husband and me. Surely you'll respect that."

"Laura!" Randall said with genuine shock.

Let Randall explain, Keely decided, moving toward the door. It was painfully clear that Laura Barlow truly believed there was something going on between her and Randall. Keely started to explain how impossible that was, then thought better of it. Surely this was something her father should be told privately. To tell him now would be to manipulate an awkward situation. Once he knew, the decision to tell or not was his alone. Of course, she could stay and help him explain the scene his wife had just interrupted…

But what came out was not an explanation. "I need to find Luke," Keely said. And fled.

As she hurried to the E.R., Luke was just entering the double doors with Matthew trotting happily beside him. Matthew spotted her and grinned and her heart turned over. He was so precious in his tiny jeans and a warm-up jacket with an Atlanta

Braves logo. Instantly the misunderstanding with the Barlows went out of her head.

"I broke my arm, Keely!" he announced proudly, hurrying toward her.

A thankful sound came from Keely as she scooped him up for a tight hug and held on in spite of the fact that he wiggled in protest. Luke watched with a half smile. Reluctantly Keely set him down.

"What happened?" she asked Luke, pushing her hair back impatiently.

"He's okay. He was horsing around with another kid and his arm was dislocated."

"It was Michael." Matthew supplied the kid's name readily. "He's six and he bet me I couldn't get to the top and when I did, he was gonna push me off, but I started to fall and he grabbed me and it really hurt!"

Keely stroked his hair. "It really does hurt when your arm is pulled out of its socket."

"Yeah! I started to cry, but Michael called me a nasty name and I quit."

"Where were the people who're supposed to prevent this sort of thing?" Keely asked Luke indignantly.

"Watching, just as they should," he said. "But stuff happens with a bunch of kids at play. It was an accident. They apologized. Over and over."

"Can I get a drink?" Matthew said. Having

milked all the drama from his "broken arm," he was eyeing two children at the water fountain.

"Yes, but wait your turn," Keely said, watching him dart away. The two children were girls, one obviously much younger than Matthew. She lowered her voice. "Is this Michael person a bully?"

Luke smiled. "No more so than any other boy who's two years older than his playmate."

She gave a skeptical huff. "Well, I think I should say something tomorrow when I drop him off."

"Maybe you should give it a day or so," he suggested. "We had a little chat on the way over here, Matthew and I, about doing things you shouldn't on a dare. He's pretty cocky at the moment, but when I got there he was scared and almost as pale as you are now. Better to let him decide on his own to steer clear of Michael. If you step in, it'll teach him another lesson, a negative one. I've seen the confidence of too many new recruits undermined by overprotective parents."

"Really."

"You don't want to teach him that when the going gets tough, Mommy will bail him out."

"He's only four years old, Luke."

He shrugged. "Okay, but that's my take on it."

Keely wanted to argue more, but she was still feeling shaky. And the way Luke was looking at her drove any desire to bicker with him out of her mind.

"He's okay, Keely," he said softly. Moving a little closer, he lifted a hand as if to touch her, then let it fall. "I wish we weren't standing here in front of everybody." His voice was low, meant for her ears only. "You look as if you need a hug as much as Matthew."

"I do." No denying that, she thought. Lost in his gaze, she put an unsteady hand on her cheek and managed a rueful laugh. "Suddenly those rules against fraternizing between employees seem stupid. I was never tempted to break them before."

"Ditto. I feel like forgetting hospital policy, too." His voice dropped even more, became a deep, intense caress. "You were scared for Matthew and nobody understands better than me. I want to wrap my arms around you and promise I won't let anything hurt him. Or you. The way I feel right now makes me want to say the hell with rules."

Her heart raced. "That would certainly cause a stir."

He touched her then, but only at her elbow to turn her toward the elevators. "C'mon, let's go home before we start tongues to wagging."

That would definitely be a problem. So far, they'd avoided tipping off the staff that their involvement was anything more than a shared, temporary effort to care for Matthew. But if anybody happened to look closely at them now, everything would change.

The hospital was like many other businesses. Personal entanglements were absolutely forbidden. And for good reasons. It was human nature for people who were personally involved to become distracted by the ups and downs of a relationship. Distraction on the part of a resident—or any caregiver—when dealing with a sick patient could result in a fatal error in judgment. Both Keely and Luke had managed to make it this far with unblemished records. The wise thing would be to keep it that way.

Keely sighed, wanting to lean against Luke as they fell into step together. She'd never felt less wise.

She looked up then, just in time to see Laura and Randall Barlow stepping from the elevator at the far end of the hall. Matthew's mishap had made her forget the incident in Randall's office. Almost. She didn't want to face that woman right now.

She grabbed Luke's arm. "Quick, let's go!" Motioning frantically, she urged him behind a large food cart.

"What?" He looked around to see what panicked her.

"Matthew!" she called in an urgent whisper. "Hurry! We've got to go home." But Matthew had waited his turn at the water fountain and he wasn't leaving without a drink.

With an exasperated sound, Keely said to Luke, "You take Matthew, okay?" Stealing a glance around the cart, she saw with relief that someone had stopped the Barlows in the hall. "I'll meet you at home."

"At which time you'll explain what the hell's going on," Luke told her with a scowl.

"Yes, yes." As she started to dash away, she gave him a look of pure distress. "But it's so bizarre you probably won't believe it."

KEELY'S CAR WAS PARKED in a distant corner of the garage, but as it was time for a shift change, there were enough people that she felt reasonably safe heading for it. Before Billy Long had entered her life, she wouldn't have had a moment's concern about where to park, but this particular corner was isolated and not well lit. Next time, she'd park illegally before settling for a remote spot like this.

She hated being forced to alter her life-style because of some perverted jerk. Now she took elaborate safety precautions at her home and when she left it, when she traveled or shopped. In a dozen ways, his intrusion into her life had wreaked havoc. It was enough to make her want to see him strung up and tortured the way he'd tortured his wife. The one thing she was thankful for was that he wasn't Matthew's biological father.

Casting a quick look around, she saw that she was essentially alone. Two rows over, tires squealed as a too-eager employee accelerated on his way out, but no one seemed to be going in her direction. Even so, she felt as if someone was watching her. A little spooked, she picked up her pace. The garage was patrolled, she reminded herself. A loud scream would bring a guard to her aid.

If she had time to scream, a tiny voice said.

Fighting paranoia, she dug in her purse for her keys. She found the electronic device which unlocked her car and placed her thumb on it. Her car seemed ten miles away, but when she finally did get there, she'd be ready.

Footsteps! She cast a fearful glance, but saw only a few stragglers, latecomers like herself who'd had to park on the outer fringes. Nobody looked in the least suspicious. She should have taken Luke's advice about getting a cell phone. Just the act of pulling out a phone and letting a stalker see it was a deterrent.

Too late now. That tiny voice again.

Panic overcame reason. She began to jog, unable to prevent another fearful look over her shoulder. In spite of the fact that she was at least forty feet from her car, she activated the electronic lock. It gave a cheerful little chirp.

Possibly a stupid move. If somebody is stalking me, now they won't have any trouble hopping into my car right beside me.

Almost there. Somewhere nearby a car door closed. A sport utility vehicle, she noted vaguely, with dark tinted windows. As she raced the last few yards to her car and jerked the door open, the driver drove away in a cloud of exhaust.

Scrambling inside, she shot a quick look over her shoulder to see that no one lurked in her back seat. She rammed the key in the ignition and, clutching the steering wheel with both hands, prepared to pull out.

Only then did she see the words smeared on her windshield.

"I'm watching you, bitch!"

CHAPTER ELEVEN

BEFORE KEELY SQUEALED TO A STOP in front of Luke's apartment, he was out the door and striding toward her. It was the new rule to go to his place if she was alone. For some added protection, Oscar was in residence.

Luke was primed to demand what that scene in the hospital had been about, but one look at her windshield made it seem trivial. As he strode toward her, Keely had her door open and almost tumbled into his arms.

"He was waiting for me in the garage, Luke!"

"Who? What happened?" Arms tight around her, he scowled at the message on her windshield, choking back a string of profanity. Controlling his tone, he asked, "Are you hurt?"

"No. No, I'm just—"

"Scared to death," he finished curtly. "Just the way he wants you."

She was trembling all over. Luke fought back fear and frustration while a wave of black rage rolled through him. The bastard was getting bolder, more reckless. If he kept it up, it was inevitable that he would make a mistake and likely the cops would get him. But would that be before or after he'd managed to get to Keely?

Goddamn it! He'd never felt so helpless.

"Did you get a look at him?" he asked, rubbing the taut muscles in her neck.

"No, but I think I saw his car." Her face was pressed to his chest, both hands clenched in a death grip on his shirt. "It had black windows."

"Tinted windows?"

"Uh-huh. I couldn't see anything. Not even the shape of him in the driver's seat. It was too dark." She drew in a shaky breath. "And I can't be certain. I just had this weird feeling that someone was watching me."

"Watching you?" Luke's tone sharpened. "Where? Where was this?"

She was beginning to calm down a little. "In the garage as I was walking to my car." She gave him the details, pulling away to tell him. Now that her panic was ebbing, she was sounding more like herself.

"Can you identify his car?"

"Only generally." Taking a deep breath, she looked toward the door of his apartment. "Is Matthew okay?"

"Matthew's fine. You're the one who needs attention right now, Keely." He began urging her up the walk to the door, keeping his arm around her. "First we have to call Detective Evans."

"I reported the incident to hospital security, which is why I'm so late, but no one saw anything."

"Evans is the one to talk to. He needs to know what you saw. It's odd, but sometimes witnesses see more than they think. The trick is getting you to remember details."

"No problem." Her voice was dry, but he felt the shudder that went through her. "I only wish I could forget."

"After you talk to Evans, darlin'." He closed the door behind them and reached for her. Her lips trembled as he kissed her, holding her close. She tasted sweet and vulnerable—Keely, vulnerable!— and he was filled with a fierce compulsion to protect her. Keely's spirit was what he'd first noticed about her. It enraged him that some scumbag had the power to do this to her.

"Where is Matthew?" she asked, tilting her head so he could get to the sensitive spot beneath her ear.

"Playing with his Lego in the bedroom."

She nodded. "Oscar's with him?"

"Of course."

She took another shaky breath and moved down the hall, where she could see for herself that Mat-

thew was okay. "This has been a really rotten
day."

"Right up there with the worst of them," he
agreed.

"You only know half of it," she said, rubbing
her forehead with two fingers. "Well, two-thirds
of it."

"What am I missing? Does it have to do with
your wild scramble to escape at the hospital?"

She looked at him. "Laura Barlow thinks I'm
having an affair with her husband."

"Come on."

She gave a helpless shrug but was not quite able
to manage a smile. "She hates me, Luke."

He held her gaze for a long moment, then
reached for the phone on the wall. "I'm calling
Detective Evans."

"Don't you want to hear this?"

"Yeah. And while he's on his way you can give
me the details."

KEELY WATCHED LUKE STIR a jar of prepared spaghetti sauce into ground beef he'd browned in a
deep-dish skillet. Years of bachelorhood had apparently forced him to learn to cook, but his culi-
nary skills didn't extend to anything complicated.
Matthew, of course, gobbled up anything Luke
produced in the kitchen.

Maybe she was selling him short, but Luke continually surprised her in his willingness to assume his share of duties around the house. She knew other married residents—and those just living together—usually had a fairly equal division of labor when it came to household chores. Keeping relationships alive while juggling demanding schedules proved too much for some. But she and Luke were not married. It could be he was thinking their situation was temporary and that he could manage to help out for a while.

For some reason, that thought depressed her.

Detective Evans had come and gone. His questions had been more or less the same ones Luke had asked. Evans pointed out that there were countless vehicles in the Atlanta area fitting the description she'd furnished. Unfortunately, without a license plate number, a be-on-the-lookout order to all law enforcement was virtually useless, he'd said. Luke demanded police protection for Keely, but Evans refused for the same reason he'd stated earlier. Until there was an overt attack, no one had broken any laws. Scrawling threatening messages on windshields was not a crime. Luke had exploded then, and although Evans was sympathetic, he was powerless.

Everyone was powerless in this bizarre situation, it seemed, except Billy Long.

While Luke filled a large pot with water to cook the spaghetti, Keely went to the refrigerator and began removing the ingredients for a salad, which she brought to the table. Before starting, she walked to the door and checked on Matthew. He was lying on the floor in front of the television. Oscar, head resting on his paws, lay close beside him. The dog glanced up and gave a friendly wag of his tail, but he made no move to leave Matthew's side to go to her.

She went back into the kitchen. "There's loyalty for you," she said, picking up a bunch of radishes. "Nothing can pry Oscar from Matthew's side now. He's apparently forgotten who feeds him, walks him and suffered through obedience class with him."

"Be thankful," Luke said. "We can't watch him twenty-four hours a day, so Oscar's the next best thing to a hired gun we've got." He sprinkled hot seasoning liberally into the spaghetti sauce. "Too bad we have to leave him at home. If you could take him with you, he'd keep Long at a distance."

"I can't, so I'll just have to be doubly on guard."

"You're getting a cell phone tomorrow."

By his tone, she knew this wasn't open to discussion and for once Keely didn't argue. Those moments in the garage were still vivid in her mind.

She went to the sink to wash the vegetables. After a moment she looked over at Luke. "So,

what do you think I should do about Laura Barlow?''

"Nothing."

"Nothing? Just let her stew over an assumption
that is completely false?''

"It's Randall's problem to fix, not yours."

"But what if she doesn't believe that nothing
happened?''

"It's still Randall's problem."

She stopped what she was doing. "You think I
should tell him, don't you?''

"That he's your father?'' He checked the pot to
see if the water was boiling. "What I think doesn't
matter. That's something you have to decide.''

"I'm going to do it."

Without comment, he dumped spaghetti into the
pot.

"Tomorrow.'' She sliced through a head of let-
tuce with a sharp knife. "I mean it.''

"Now that you've stopped bugging Laura about
taking Matthew, it removes one complication…if
you should decide to tell him,'' he added.

"You're right. She just isn't the right person to
be Matthew's mother.''

Luke was smiling as he tossed a wooden spoon
into the sink. "I have a feeling not even Mother
Teresa would have met your standards for Matthew's mother, darlin'.''

She looked at him. "It's just that Matthew's had

so many bad breaks in his life that we have to be right the first time. We don't want him getting attached to someone who then decides to abandon him. First his father, then his mother, you, me…all he's known in his short life is abandonment.''

''Yeah, it's tough.''

With a resigned look, she began wiping off the tabletop. ''I suppose adoption is the logical answer.''

''Adoption.'' His amusement disappeared.

''And we're going to scrutinize the adoptive parents down to the style of their underwear, Luke. If there's anything…I mean *anything* in their background that even *hints* at instability or…or abuse or—''

''I get the picture.'' Luke covered the simmering spaghetti sauce and turned, resting his hips against the kitchen counter. ''Couples like that are hard to find.''

She sighed, pausing with sponge in hand. ''I know.'' Then, not looking at him, she added, ''Unless a certain dedicated second-year resident and his admiring third-year resident superior would consider taking it on.''

''Are we a couple?''

After a beat of silence, she lifted her gaze to his. ''Aren't we?''

He waited a little too long to reply. Keely threw

the sponge in the direction of the sink. "I don't know, Luke. You tell me." Her tone was very soft.

"We're seeing each other exclusively, we're sleeping together. Yeah. I guess that makes us a couple." He looked uncomfortable.

"But only once, Luke," she said, propping herself against the opposite counter and facing him. "We slept together only once. And you're right. I shouldn't have assumed that makes us a couple. And, sure as heck, no judge would say it qualifies us to adopt a child. I don't know what I could have been thinking of to even mention it."

What was she doing? What was she saying? She sounded like a woman trying to push a reluctant man-friend into making a commitment he wasn't ready for. Had she lost her mind?

Luke pushed away from the counter and shoved his hands into his pockets. "I know what you're getting at. Matthew needs the stability of marriage. You're right about that." He went to the hall as if checking on the little boy. "And sure, we're a couple. We're together, but…not together. You know what I mean."

"I definitely do now," she said. She turned abruptly and took down three plates. "Forget I even brought that up, Luke. It sounded like a pitch to get you to the altar and we both know we're not headed in that direction."

He turned and looked at her. "I think we should

just keep on as we're doing...for the time being, you know?''

"For Matthew's sake, I don't think we have much choice...for the time being," she added with derision. She plunked the plates down on the table, one at a time. "But don't be surprised if there are a few changes."

"Like what?"

"Come on, Luke."

"You were as willing as I was last night, Keely."

"A person can be mistaken."

He drove frustrated fingers through his hair. "It's stupid to even have this discussion right now. What's so urgent that we have to settle the question of the future tonight? And why does the question of adoption even have to come up? As you've said more than once, Matthew's had a lot of change in just a few short weeks. Besides, Evans is still trying to find his father. All this could be irrelevant if he decides he wants Matthew. And there's still Billy Long to consider. Until he's in custody, there's no way I'd feel safe turning Matthew over to some faceless adoption agency."

"You know I don't want to do that!" Keely took a deep breath, then spoke with less heat. "I'm just trying to figure out what's best. I don't like when I'm faced with all these...uncertainties."

He came up behind her, but didn't touch her. He

spoke quietly. "It's going to be okay. It'll all work out."

"Matthew's not like a pet you can bring home from the store and keep for a while to see if you like him," she said in a shaky voice. "He's a little boy and he deserves a home. A real home with real parents. One way or another, I'm going to see that he gets that."

"I'm with you there, Keely. You know that."

But not if it means marriage. Maybe it would work out as Luke seemed to believe. She hoped it would. Prayed it would. As they stood, nearly touching but now so far apart, she heard the theme from *Sesame Street.* Matthew loved Elmo. One of the first things she'd bought him had been a soft, snuggly version of the bright red character. He slept with it, ate with it, sat it on the toilet while he took his bath. Would his adoptive parents be sensitive to the fears of a little boy who'd just lost his mother? Or would they be eager to erase all ties with his past? Was Luke right? *Was* she being too sensitive worrying about it? Would everything work out for Matthew?

Last night, enveloped in Luke's strength, caught up in his passion, it had been easy to feel reassured about Matthew, at least. But the past few minutes had dimmed her bright expectations of any future they might have together. Luke clearly wasn't interested in marriage.

AFTER A RESTLESS NIGHT, Keely went to the hospital early, leaving Luke to drop Matthew off at day care. She'd gone to bed in Matthew's room last night. The more she thought about Luke's reluctance to commit himself to her, the more worked up she became. Was she just a convenient sex partner? Was sleeping with her merely a perk that came with his willingness to share responsibility for Matthew? The idea had never crossed her mind until they'd stumbled into the discussion last night and he was so clearly not ready to talk about it. Or not willing. Was she the only one who had fallen in love? Oh, Lord, that was truly scary.

So what did she want now? She wanted to be married...eventually. Like most women, her plans for the future included a husband, children, career—always had. It was unsettling to find that she might not be able to keep those plans on a back burner until a more convenient time. Matthew was here right now. Luke was in her life right now. Uncertainties again. And that made her nervous, edgy.

But there was one uncertainty in her life that she could handle today. At the hospital, she went directly to Randall's office. A therapist would probably explain that her need for order and structure stemmed from a childhood without either. She was realistic enough to know that no one could control all aspects of life always. Stuff happened, just look at Phyllis Long and Matthew. At least, on the subject of her relationship to Randall and Laura's wrongheaded suspicions, she could do something.

She knocked on his door, pushing it open when he told her to come in. "Got a minute?" she asked, standing in the doorway.

He smiled. "For you, Keely? Always."

She was shaking her head as she sat down in the chair and faced him. "You may change your mind once you hear what I have to say."

He sobered instantly. "If it's about Laura jumping to such a ridiculous conclusion yesterday, please accept my apology. I explained what happened to Laura. She can understand how emotional one gets when one's child is hurt."

"Matthew isn't my child, Randall."

He gave her a chiding look. "Isn't he?"

She let that pass. "You say Laura understands why I was upset, but did you convince her that her…suspicions otherwise are so wrong?"

"She'll come around."

With a sigh, Keely sat back in her chair. "This is so…bizarre."

"Is it really? Consider yourself through Laura's eyes. You're a beautiful young woman, a gifted physician well on the way to a specialty in emergency medicine. You're at life's doorway, ready to sample everything it has to offer. You'll marry, have children, a career, all of which you'll manage well. Is it so extraordinary for my wife to imagine that my feelings for you might go beyond simple admiration?"

"Yes!" she cried. "She should trust you!"

Smiling, Randall studied her for a moment.

"Thank you." Then his smile faded as he gazed at the photos displayed on a credenza. Keely watched his face as he looked at his daughter. Shelley at six in an Easter outfit, grinning and showing a missing tooth as she held up a basket of colored eggs. Shelley at twelve—a tomboy in a baseball cap worn backward. Shelley at seventeen in cap and gown for her high school graduation.

"Laura's heart is broken, you know," he said. "Losing Shelley at such a young age, her life just beginning…"

But at least Shelley knew you for seventeen years. She pushed that unworthy thought aside. "Not just Laura. It must have been terrible for you both."

"Devastating. I was full of rage for a while. I'd counseled hundreds of people who'd lost loved ones, but all my wise—" he made quotation marks with his fingers "—words were utterly meaningless. It was *my* child this time, *my* life turned upside down, *my* grief and bewilderment and loss." His gaze moved back to Keely. "It was a dark time."

"I'm so sorry."

He nodded and looked away thoughtfully. After a moment, he said, "I've lost two children in my life."

"Two?" She frowned.

"Yes. Shelley was taken by God, but I destroyed the other."

He had picked up his pen and Keely saw that

his hand was unsteady. Her own heart was beating like a trapped bird. Could he be talking about her?

"It was a long time ago." He dropped the pen and rubbed a spot between his eyes. "I was young, reckless. I was the spoiled, rebellious son of a minister doing everything I could to reject the traditions and morals of my parents." He gave a humorless laugh. "I was a heartless fool."

Was her chance being handed to her so easily? "Did this..." Keely swallowed. "Did this happen in New Orleans?"

"Yes, that's where I grew up."

"I know. I remember. You told me." She looked right into his eyes. "But I already knew. My mother told me about you."

"Told you—" Randall stopped, studied her face with a confused look.

"My mother's name is Tessa. She was Tessa Sheldon then."

All the color drained from his face. "Keely..." He breathed her name in shock. "What...what year were you born?"

She told him, then managed a shaky smile. "You lost only one daughter, Randall. My mother never got that abortion."

"Oh, my God." He stood up abruptly, sending his chair slamming back into the credenza. Now he was looking at her as if he'd never seen her before. Keely knew he was searching for a likeness, some similarity to someone in his family. Wondering if it could possibly be.

She stood, too. "I'm sorry. I've tried to think how best to tell you... Are you all right?"

He was still inspecting her features, his gaze roving hungrily over her face, her hair, her hands. "I should have known," he murmured, not to her, but to himself.

"I have your eyes," she told him.

"Dear God."

She smiled. "You said that."

"Tessa didn't have the abortion," he repeated, stunned.

"No."

He closed his eyes. "Thank you."

She wasn't sure who he was thanking. God? Tessa? Her for telling? As she watched, he moved from behind the desk like a man in a dream. "Can I...I mean, could I hug you?"

"Only if Laura isn't just outside that door."

With a broken laugh, he swept her up in his arms, holding her as if he'd never let go. She sensed he was close to tears and her own emotions tightened her throat. His embrace was wonderful. Never having known the loving arms of a father, Keely basked in the moment. She clung to him, let her tears flow, took in the wondrous fact that he was happy to know her.

He let her go, except for her hands, which he held tight and fast in his own. "How is your mother?"

"She's great. She's happy. She does wonderful things for troubled kids."

"Even then I knew she had a good heart. Better than mine."

"She's a twin, you know."

"Yes, Stephanie, isn't it? How is she?"

"Great. Also very happy. She's a physician."

He was gazing at her fondly. "So you have two powerful role models."

"Sometimes I think they're a little too powerful." She grinned. "Then I get over it."

"You have no siblings?"

"There's only me."

Impulsively he hugged her again. "Oh, Keely. My daughter. It's almost too good to be true." Taking her hand, he urged her back into the chair and sat down in the one beside it. "You've been here three years. Why didn't you say something before?"

"It isn't always welcome news to some people that they have a child they never knew about."

"But surely you knew I wasn't that kind of person?" Behind his question, she sensed his hurt.

She nodded. "I did know that, but as I was working up my courage Shelley died."

"And maybe you were wise, at the time." Some of the joy faded from his eyes. "I don't know how I would have reacted then. The same as today, I think. I hope. But for both of us, Laura and I, it was a terrible time."

"I could see that," Keely said, then shrugged helplessly. "And time just…passed, one year, then another. Somehow I never seemed to find the right moment." Looking down, she began tracing the stitching on her lab coat. "But after Laura's misguided assumption yesterday, I had to say something. For me," she added, meeting his eyes. "This doesn't need to go any further, Randall." She stopped when he put up a hand. "What?"

"I guess it's too soon to call me Dad, huh?"

"You mean out loud?" She was smiling. "I've been calling you Dad in my head for three years."

He took her hand in his and kissed it. "I can't believe this! It's a miracle. It's the best Christmas present I could have…ever! I don't know how I'll be able to keep it to myself." He looked at her. "Do I have to keep it to myself?"

"That's for you to decide."

Some of his exuberance faded. "You're thinking of Laura."

"Yes. She may not be as pleased as you appear to be."

He held on to her hand. "I don't just appear to be pleased, dear girl. I can't think of anything that could please me more."

"So you will tell Laura?"

"Yes, of course."

Keely wished she felt as sure as he sounded.

"Be careful, okay? It's a lot to lay on her all of a sudden. Yesterday she believed me to be a rival for your affection and today I'm your daughter, instead. Her stepdaughter."

"She'll come around."

Again she failed to share his confidence. "You keep saying that and so does Luke."

"Luke knows?"

"I... Yes, he knows."

His eyes twinkled. "I suppose I have a rival for your affections now, don't I?"

"What do you mean?" But she knew and inwardly gave a groan.

"Keely." He was amused. "One look at the two of you together and Laura wouldn't have entertained the silly notion she did for one second. She would have seen for herself that you're in love with her nephew."

"I'm not—" But she saw on his face that it was a waste of time to deny it. She dropped her head into her hand. "Is it that obvious?"

"Only to someone who knows you both," he said. Then he added soothingly, "You've been very discreet."

"Oh, sure. So much so that you nailed it right away."

He laughed out loud. "Ministers are supposed to be intuitive that way." Then he groaned. "Lis-

ten to me. If I'm so intuitive, why did I not have
a clue as to who you really are?''

"Because you never had cause to believe I existed.''

He sobered. "I'm so sorry. I must get in touch
with Tessa and tell her that this has weighed on
my conscience for years."

She patted his hand. "In time. Let's not do anything right now, okay?"

"Laura first, huh?" Turning his hand, he
squeezed hers and again kissed it.

"Laura first.''

CHAPTER TWELVE

LUKE ENTERED THE PLAY YARD at day care and frowned over the crowd of noisy, rambunctious preschoolers. Usually Matthew sensed when it was time for him to be picked up and once he spotted Keely or Luke, he quickly separated from the group. But he was nowhere in sight today.

It was lousy timing that had Luke scheduled to work a thirty-six-hour shift starting tomorrow morning and going straight through Friday when he wanted to be patching things up with Keely. He'd decided his best bet was to take her to bed, where the chances of them coming to some understanding were best.

Things had been strained between them since that unsettling conversation about marriage. He was afraid she was working up to asking him to bow out of looking after Matthew. And once she did that, she would withdraw from him. The only good thing about this whole Billy Long situation was that it kept Keely close. She needed him, but he didn't want to be needed just that way. He wanted her in his bed and sitting across the breakfast table and juggling Matthew's schedule and arguing with him and in a dozen other ways...but especially in his bed. Even though the thought of marriage still made him sweat.

A soccer ball came shooting across the lawn and Luke swept it up, tossing it back to a bunch of little boys. There was still no sign of Matthew.

At least, Keely understood the drawbacks to his career. His own E.R. rotation was winding down, and he'd soon move to another in Oncology where duty wasn't so hectic. And where he wouldn't see nearly as much of Keely. Her specialty was Trauma, so she would stay in the E.R. What happened after he rotated depended on how he fixed what went wrong. He might be leery of marriage, but he definitely didn't want Keely to walk out of his life.

Noisy shouts caught his attention and he zeroed in on a rowdy group at the jungle gym. Two kids fighting, he realized, both going at it tooth and nail.

"Matthew," he muttered, recognizing the Braves logo on one boy's jacket. Smothering a profanity, he started across the play yard at a rapid clip at the same time as a day-care worker dashed over to break it up.

Luke reached the scene as Chrissie—he remembered her name from the last episode—was pulling the boys apart, both still swinging. Matthew sported a small cut on his chin and the beginning of a fine shiner beneath his left eye. He'd look like a small, battered raccoon tomorrow, Luke thought. "What's going on here?" he demanded.

"Apparently a disagreement between the boys, Dr. Jamison," Chrissie said, giving them both a stern look. "And they know fighting is not the way we resolve differences here."

Luke tipped Matthew's sullen face up to get a good look and saw instantly that the cut would require a stitch. He glanced at the other boy. "I guess this must be Michael," he said to Matthew.

"Uh-huh," Matthew mumbled.

"Want to tell us what this was all about?"

"He said stuff that made me mad," Matthew said, darting a resentful look at his playmate.

"He hit me first!" Michael cried.

"Because you said mean stuff!"

"Okay, okay, guys." Luke gave Chrissie an apologetic look. "I'm sorry about this. Keely and I will be in tomorrow to settle things, but right now I'm going to have to take Matthew to the E.R."

Chrissie looked alarmed. "Do you think that's necessary?"

"He's going to require a stitch in that chin."

"No!" Matthew's lip quivered. "I don't want any stitches."

"It'll be okay, son. Keely's on duty now. She'll do it."

"Will it hurt?"

"Only a little."

Matthew was not reassured, but he allowed Luke to use the wet-wipe towel given to him by another attendant and gently cleanse the wound on his chin. A stitch was definitely required. The shiner was also blooming nicely. Luke straightened. Keely was going to freak out.

He put a hand on the boy's shoulder. "Before we leave, how about you two shaking hands?"

"Uh-uh," Matthew said, still scowling.

"No way," Michael returned with matching hostility.

Chrissie gave a rueful shrug. "Dr. Jamison, I don't think—"

Luke put his other hand on Michael's shoulder and firmly turned both boys so that they faced each other. "I know you guys don't want to hear a lecture right now, so I'm going to make this short and sweet and then I expect you to shake hands like gentlemen. You've had a disagreement, and you've resorted to fighting to settle it, but you're both still mad. Tomorrow when you come to school, it'll be more fun to play together than to sulk and hold a grudge." He gave each of them a small prod. "Now, shake!"

It was Michael, not Matthew, who finally stuck out his hand. Matthew, his face as dark as a thundercloud, reluctantly did likewise.

"That's better." Luke released the boys and

Matthew instantly turned and ran toward the car. "I think a time-out tomorrow might be a good idea for both of these guys," Luke suggested. "They need to be reminded that resorting to violence has unpleasant consequences."

She smiled. "Absolutely. And we'll have a lesson for the whole group on the subject."

Matthew was waiting at the Explorer, looking anything but repentant. Climbing into the front seat, he silently fastened his seat belt. After Luke got in, he tipped up the boy's chin to examine the cut once more before settling back and starting the car. "What did Michael say that set you off?"

Matthew crossed his small arms over his chest and scowled. "Just some stuff."

"Mean stuff."

"Uh-huh."

Shifting into drive, Luke pulled away from the day-care complex. Obviously Matthew wasn't going to volunteer what happened. Luke would leave it up to Keely to drag the facts from the little boy. Encouraging communication was her area of expertise, not Luke's. It surprised him when the little boy spoke again.

"Michael said heaven is just a make-believe place."

"You and Michael were talking about heaven?"

"Yeah." Matthew picked at a scratch on one knuckle.

Luke waited.

The boy turned in his seat. "He's wrong, isn't he?"

Luke wished he knew what they were really talking about. "Just because you can't see something doesn't mean it isn't real."

"He said angels aren't real, either."

"Hmm, that was some serious stuff you two were discussing."

"Yeah."

Luke glanced in the rearview mirror before turning at the hospital. "What did Michael say that was really mean?"

"Something about my mommy."

Suddenly understanding came to Luke. He tried to recall if the kids at day care knew anything about Matthew's background. He thought not, but you could never tell what kids picked up. Matthew surprised him all the time.

"My mommy's in heaven, isn't she?" the boy asked anxiously.

"Yes, your mommy's in heaven," Luke said, without hesitation. Had Michael—the little creep—said otherwise?

"And she's an angel, isn't she?"

Luke's beliefs about heaven and hell and angels were pretty murky. He was open to things spiritual, but he wasn't about to go there with a little kid whose mother had been murdered just a couple of weeks ago.

"Why are you asking that? Did Michael say that your mommy wasn't an angel?"

"Yeah."

Mean-spirited little jerk. Luke drove up the curved driveway to the E.R. a little too fast and stopped with a squeal of his brakes. "I believe your mommy's an angel, Matthew," he said, realizing he meant it.

"You do?" The little boy was studying him intently.

"Yeah, I do. She was a nice lady, a good person. And those are the people who make the best angels."

Matthew thought that over, then nodded. "That's what I thought, too."

"Now…" Luke reached for the door handle. "Let's take care of that chin, buddy."

LUKE LEFT MATTHEW SITTING in one of the treatment cubicles being entertained by Jenny Blackwell while he went in search of Keely. Any one of the E.R. residents could have stitched the cut on Matthew's chin, himself included, but Luke knew Keely would want to do it. He found her supervising a first-year resident who was treating a young male for a gunshot wound in the shoulder.

"His mother says he was shot in the groin six

months ago,'' Keely told the nervous resident, who was gingerly probing into the wound with a finger trying to find the bullet. "I remember him...." It had been a gang dispute over a girl.

She glanced up as Luke pulled the curtain back. She and a male nurse each held an arm, forcing the patient to hold still. "And here's Dr. Jamison, who performed the first surgery."

Luke looked at the victim, who was fighting the oxygen mask and the efforts of the resident to try to save his life. "He's high."

Keely sighed. "And scared."

"He was high and scared the first time," Luke said with a disgusted look. "But apparently not enough to get out of that gang the way he promised his mother."

Keely tilted her head questioningly. "Did you pick up Matthew?"

"Yeah, a few minutes ago."

She frowned. "Where is he?"

"He's here, in a treatment cubicle. He got in a fight with Michael and he's going to need a stitch in—"

"Stitches!" Keely started to move away but was stopped by the resident's alarmed look.

"I'll take over here," Luke said, reaching for rubber gloves. "Matthew wants you to do the stitching."

"Where?"

"Cubicle six."

She shook her head impatiently. "I mean where does he need stitches? What happened? Why did the day-care attendants let this happen?" Stripping off her gloves, she tossed them into the waste bin. "You aren't talking me out of it this time, Luke. I'm speaking to them about this. First his arm is dislocated, now it's stitches."

"The shiner won't need anything but an ice pack," Luke said, deadpan.

"Shiner!"

He nodded toward the hall. "Cubicle six."

AN HOUR LATER, Keely left the hospital with Matthew. The little boy didn't seem any worse for the injuries he'd suffered at the hands of that bully, but Keely was still seething over it. And she disagreed with Luke that the episodes of violence were natural for a child in Matthew's circumstances. The way Luke saw it, Matthew was the new kid at day care, and he thought it was normal to resolve differences with aggression. So when Michael had taunted him, he'd attacked. He could be excused for feeling bewildered and overwhelmed, Luke claimed. Taking him away from day care and forcing him to adjust to yet another new situation wasn't a good idea just now.

She sighed. Was Luke right? Was she overreacting? And what other option did she have except day care? She had no guarantee that he would be better off in another facility.

Having full responsibility for a four-year-old child was proving more complicated than simply making room for him in her busy life. That was difficult enough. Today, for instance, she'd been on for only nine hours of a thirty-six-hour shift when Matthew had been hurt. She'd had to arrange for someone to cover for her, at least until tomorrow morning. Maybe she wasn't Matthew's biological mother, but she certainly felt as if she were. Like any concerned parent, she wanted to take him home and fuss over him a little—which reminded her of the discussion with Luke about adoption and commitment and relationships. She might have been offended by his reaction, but he was probably right in realizing how difficult it would be to adjust her life-style to accommodate a young child. Unfortunately, there were no easy answers.

"I was pretty brave, wasn't I, Keely?" Matthew said. Holding her hand, he looked up at her as they headed for her car. The windshield incident yesterday had shaken her. Not knowing she'd be getting off early, she'd parked her car in one of the assistant chaplain slots. With her father's approval.

Her father. Joy replaced her somber mood.

"You didn't answer me, Keely."

"I'm sorry, honey bun. I was thinking. And yes,

you were the bravest little boy I've stitched up in a long time.''

"How many boys have you stitched up?''

"Oh, dozens.''

"Is that a lot?''

"It's a lot, and you're the bravest.'' She squeezed his hand as they approached her car. Using the remote, she popped the electric locks and opened the door for Matthew on the passenger side. Boosting him onto the seat, she reminded him to buckle up, then closed the door and headed around the back of the car to get to the driver's side.

She noticed then that the overhead security light was out. Everything that happened next seemed to be a slow-motion nightmare. A man rose from the thick landscaping and before she could react one way or another, he was coming at her. He was huge. His clothes were dark and he wore a baseball cap. His face…she realized she couldn't see his face, but she knew who it was. Like a kick in the stomach, she knew Billy Long had found her at last. She thought of Matthew, small and vulnerable, buckled in the front seat.

Please don't let him take Matthew.

Terror gave birth to a scream as he flung her savagely onto the concrete. Her hands flew out instinctively to break her fall, but she still hit the rough pavement hard, banging her head and scraping her cheek. She felt pain as her knee hit, and she curled into herself in a futile effort to protect herself. Then more pain as he kicked her in the side. Was he going to kill her?

She screamed again as he bent low and grabbed a handful of hair, then wrenched it back viciously. He caught her face with his other hand in a cruel grip and looked right into her eyes.

"You killed my wife, you bitch!"

But his words seemed to come from far away. Pain made it hard to concentrate. "Don't hurt Matthew," she begged, putting up a hand as he struck a blow that stunned her.

Then, at the sound of a shout, he let her go abruptly. Her head fell back on the curb and stars exploded in a bright shower. For a second or two he stood over her, cursing, then he aimed a final, painful kick that would have hit her abdomen had she not rolled slightly and caught the blow on her thigh instead. Then he turned and ran, disappearing into the dark sea of cars.

From a distance she heard voices and realized weakly that he probably would have killed her but for the unexpected arrival of another person. She tried vainly to get up.

And then someone was beside her.

"Keely, Keely, dear one, little girl…" It was her father's voice. She was trembling now, trying to hold herself together.

"M-Matthew," she whispered.

"He's in the car," Randall told her, ripping his jacket off and shoving it beneath her head. "He's safe."

"Did he...see? I don't want him to see this."

"I don't think he saw anything. He was belted in and facing the other way." Randall groped for her hand. "Lie still, dear. Help is on the way."

"He—he broke the security light," she said, blinking up at the vacant socket high above her.

"Yes."

Someone in green scrubs was there suddenly. Steve Langdon, she thought, a second-year resident in obstetrics. "I'm not pregnant, Steve," she said with a weak smile.

"No, but we OB types are good for other stuff, too. Just lie still and let me check you out, babe."

Another flurry of footsteps and somebody else was elbowing Steve aside. "Keely!" It was Luke. "Damn it!" He was down on the pavement beside her, his hands moving over her frantically.

"Don't swear in front of Matthew," she whispered, feeling a soft darkness beginning to descend. She was going to pass out. Luke would want her to fight it. First rule: keep the patient conscious, if possible. But it wasn't possible. Sounds were already receding. She focused on Luke's face.

He was scared, she realized, seeing the fear in his eyes. She wanted to reach up and touch his cheek, his mouth. She wanted to tell him not to worry, but her arm was too heavy to obey her brain.

"Stay with me, sweetheart!" he ordered, holding her face in his hands and forcing her to look at him.

"I...hurt," she managed to say, just a whisper of sound.

"I'll take care of you."

"And M-Matthew..." Her lashes were so heavy. Too heavy.

"And Matthew," he repeated. "Always." But she was out.

Luke looked up desperately into Randall's eyes. Words teemed on his tongue—prayers, demands, curses. He saw understanding on Randall's face and the same fear. Turning back to Keely, his training kicked in. If she were supervising and saw him in this shape, she'd dress him down without mercy. Rising, he yelled to a male aide across the Tarmac. "Get a gurney over here. Fast!"

RANDALL ZAPPED THE GARAGE DOOR with a remote and pulled his Buick inside, stopping beside Laura's car. After killing the motor, he simply sat at the wheel wondering what he'd find when he went inside. He was shaken to the core by the brutal attack on Keely, and Luke's reaction had been just as strong. But it was Matthew whose fear had been heart wrenching.

Although the little boy hadn't seen anything, he'd been badly frightened by the commotion. And as soon as he'd realized Keely had been hurt, he'd tumbled out of the car and rushed to her side, terrified. Luke had taken a few precious moments to reassure the boy as Keely was lifted onto a gurney to be rushed into the E.R. It was plain as day, whether Luke realized it or not, that Matthew had become far more to him than just a little boy who temporarily needed him for food and shelter.

Knowing Keely would reject any other option, Luke had turned to Randall as the only logical person to take care of Matthew. Randall had readily agreed. When he'd brought the boy home, Laura had been shocked to learn of the attack and had willingly agreed to care for Matthew while Keely recovered. She'd even agreed to have the dog, Oscar. The little boy had been wary and anxious at first, but Randall had finally managed to distract him with cartoons.

He'd then settled in to wait for a report on Keely, but had been unable to sit still. He'd called the hospital and been told Luke was with her and someone would call him soon with a progress report. He'd thought of trying to explain his extreme concern to Laura, but he needed to be in a calmer

state to handle such a delicate task. Laura had finally snapped at him to go to the hospital.

"I know that's where you want to be," she'd
said in a huff. "Don't worry about Matthew. I'll
take care of him."

"I'll be back as soon as I get a status report,"
he'd promised her, grabbing at the chance to see
Keely for himself.

She'd turned away. "Well, don't rush back on
my account."

Now he sat in his car, reluctant to go into the
house and wishing he knew how she would react
when he told her what was on his mind. And in
his heart.

He entered the kitchen from the garage and was
met by Keely's big Lab. He spoke softly to the
dog and closed the door. All was quiet except for
the sound of Christmas carols coming from the in-
tercom on the wall. Two cups with chocolate stains
sat in the sink, a sign that his wife and Matthew
were getting along. He was glad Laura had apparently managed to persuade Matthew to drink hot
chocolate. He had refused anything to eat or drink
when they'd first gotten to the house.

The family room was partially visible from the
breakfast bar dividing it from the kitchen, but it
was empty. The television was off and the soft
glow from the Christmas tree was the only light in
the room. If Laura and Matthew were upstairs, he

hoped that meant the little boy was asleep. He headed toward the tree to turn the lights out.

"Don't. Not yet."

It was his wife's voice, and it came from the shadowy corner near the fireplace.

"Leave them on," she said in a soft tone.

He stared in speechless surprise. Laura sat in a rocking chair that had been retired several years ago, a rocking chair used daily when Shelley was a baby. The big Lab stood on guard beside the chair. In his wife's arms, Matthew slept peacefully, the squeak of the rockers mixing gently with the sweet strains of the old carol, *"What Child is This?"* She was quietly weeping.

He started toward her. "Laura…"

"He fell asleep only a few minutes ago," she said, tenderly stroking his blond head. "He was so worried about his…about Keely. He's afraid she won't come back for him."

Randall was beside the chair now. "She will. She's shaken up and bruised, but nothing's broken."

Laura looked into the sleeping boy's face. "Nothing I said would convince him he'd ever see her again."

"He never saw his mother after she was a victim of a violent attack," Randall explained, his gaze fixed on his wife's tearful face. "His fear of abandonment is natural."

"I went upstairs and got the rocking chair."

A smile lit his eyes. "Apparently a good idea."

"He just needed—" her voice broke "—somebody to h-hold him, I think."

Randall touched her knee. "I'm glad you sensed that."

She closed her eyes and rested her head back against the old-fashioned chair, her tears running unchecked down her cheeks. "I'm sorry I've been so...so closed to the idea of helping this little boy, Randall."

"You're helping him now."

"If I hadn't been so stubborn, he wouldn't have a black eye and stitches in his chin."

"He's certainly all boy."

"I didn't think I could bear being around a child," she said with a beseeching look in her eyes. "Can you understand that?"

"I do understand, darling. I always did. I just wish I'd been able to ease the ache in your heart."

She opened her eyes and looked at him. "The strange thing is that once I held him close, the ache in my heart was—"

"Gone?"

"No, not gone. Only not quite so unbearable."

"I'm glad."

Matthew suddenly shifted, rubbing at his nose with a small fist as if to remove a tickle, then turned in Laura's arms and snuggled closer, clutching a soft, brown teddy bear under one arm. In seconds, he was again sleeping deeply.

"He seems very contented there," Randall observed in a husky tone.

For a moment, both simply watched the child sleep. Then Laura spoke. "Would you get me a tissue from that box on the coffee table, please?"

Randall rose, pulled several out and gave them to her. "Shall I take him upstairs?"

She nodded, mopping her eyes. "I've fixed him a bed in the guest room. He watched me put on the sheets and reminded me that he needed his Elmo. Unfortunately, in the confusion after the…the attack today, Elmo was somehow misplaced. That's when he began to cry."

Randall realized the little brown teddy bear could not possibly be Elmo. He looked questioningly into Laura's eyes.

"It was Shelley's," she said simply.

A milestone. Across the hall from the guest room, the door to Shelley's room had remained closed for two years. No matter how Randall had urged Laura to open it up, everything in it was just as it had been on the day their daughter died. Now a small brown teddy bear was missing from her collection. Definitely a milestone.

Clearing the emotion from his throat, he said, "How about I take him upstairs and we try to put him to bed?"

"Yes."

Randall bent and carefully lifted Matthew from her arms, then followed her up the stairs to the guest room while Oscar trotted behind. He lay Matthew down, then watched as the boy drew himself up into a tiny ball and snuggled into the pillow, one arm still tight around the teddy bear, the dog curled up on the rug beside the bed.

"He'll want a night-light, I imagine," Laura said, turning a switch on a small lamp with a Beatrix Potter scene on it. Another of Shelley's possessions.

After a moment, they turned and left the room together.

HALF AN HOUR LATER, Laura was sitting up in bed when Randall came out of the shower. She removed her glasses and set her diary aside, marking her place with a ribbon. "Do they have any idea who attacked your friend?"

Randall stood for a moment looking at his wife in a soft, lacy blue gown. What he said now—how he said it—would mark a turning point in their marriage. The hard feelings and mistrust of the past few weeks might only seem like a prologue when Laura heard what he had to tell. He was surprised how moved he'd been by her tears earlier. For a little while, he'd glimpsed the Laura he loved, the mother of his child, the companion whose com-

pany and conversation, whose support and understanding he had always counted on.

At forty-two, she was still a beautiful woman.
Tonight her beauty stirred his desire. For the first
time in weeks, he wanted to make love with his
wife. But deep in his belly, anxiety was building.
He moved around to her side of the bed and sat
down. "Keely is not my friend, Laura."

He saw fear leap into her eyes and immediately
rushed to correct her misunderstanding. "Wait,
that didn't come out right. Keely is my friend, certainly. You know that. But there's something else
I need to tell you."

She turned her face from him, lips trembling. "I
don't want to know any more."

Catching her shoulders, he gave her a little
shake. "Listen to me! I'm trying to tell you something that I just learned today, something that has
changed my life. Something that will change *our*
lives."

"You want a divorce because you're in love
with her."

He sighed. "No, Laura. How could I be in love
with her when I love you, more now than I did
when we married? More than I can ever say?" He
shook his head in genuine bewilderment. "How
could you even think such a thing?"

There were tears in her eyes again. "What
then?"

"I have to go back a few years," he told her. "Back to my sixteenth year. I was the stereotypical son of a preacher. My parents prayed that I would choose the ministry as a profession, but to me that wasn't even an option. I thought I'd been born to raise hell, not to raise peoples' consciousness."

"That's hardly uncommon, is it?" Laura said. "Other ministers' wives have shared similar stories about their husbands who were sons of ministers. It's just a phase."

"Maybe," Randall said. "But before I got through that phase, I got a girl pregnant."

"Oh."

"I gave her money to get an abortion."

Laura's eyes went wide. "Oh, no."

He gave a rueful laugh. "Don't worry. She didn't do it." He still held his wife's hand and was rubbing his thumb slowly back and forth over her soft skin. "She took the money. She left New Orleans and she had the baby."

"And you never knew?" Laura whispered in shock.

"No, I never knew, but I never forgot, either. That act has weighed on my conscience for years."

"So, how—? When did you—?"

Now was the moment to lay everything on the line. "I have a daughter, Laura. She's twenty-eight years old. She lives right here in Atlanta."

"I don't understand." The fear had returned to

her eyes as if the details were going to be too much. Then her voice changed. She looked at him and spoke with deadly calm. "Do we know her?"

"We know her," he said. "It's Keely."

CHAPTER THIRTEEN

LUKE'S EXPRESSION, as he studied her chart, was unreadable. Keely watched him, wondering whether she'd have to chastise him about his awkward bedside skills even as he was treating her. No, that wasn't fair. In spite of his underwhelming efforts, she'd seen some improvement in the past two of his six-week E.R. rotation. Not that she was going to tell him that. If he sensed any softening in her, he'd eat her alive.

He made a notation and returned the chart to the holder on the wall before picking up the IV line that dangled from a plastic bag above her head. Seeing the hypodermic in his hand, she realized he was going to inject medication into her IV, probably a narcotic.

"What are you doing?"

"Just adding a little something to make you feel better."

"I feel fine," she said, ignoring the jackhammer in her brain. Actually, she suffered dire consequences every time she moved her head. It hurt like the devil.

''You'll feel even better in about two minutes.''

''I don't need it,'' she told him, but her tone lacked her usual conviction.

''Humor me.''

She could feel the strange rush as the drug entered her bloodstream, and fought it. She didn't want to be vulnerable around Luke. It would undermine her determination to end things between them. Loving him as she did, she wasn't willing to set herself up for heartbreak. And she wasn't up for an affair when mostly all he felt for her was sexual attraction. Oh, he cared for her. And she knew it had upset him to see her battered and bruised on the pavement, but he was first and foremost a physician. He was supposed to care about people.

Now he was gently parting her hair to inspect the bump on the side of her head. No bandage had been required since the skin was not broken, but it had been a hard knock. She sighed and allowed her eyes to close because it was comforting to be pampered by Luke. She could allow herself that little perk after being mugged, couldn't she?

He lifted her hospital gown to check the bruise near her kidney. ''Turn a little bit, can you, sweetheart?'' She heard him smother a curse and knew the damage must be ugly.

''That's where he kicked me.''

"I can see that," Luke said. His hands were gentle, but his tone was as hard as nails.

"I thought I'd passed out," she said. Moving carefully, she struggled to get up on one elbow to see for herself in spite of her dizziness.

"You did pass out," Luke said, pressing her back on the bed.

"Only after he dropped me on my head on the curb. And only briefly."

"Bastard…"

The truth was, her first clear memory after the attack did not come at the scene, but in the E.R. She'd come around feeling as if she'd been hit head-on by a train. Vaguely she'd heard Luke's voice urging her to lie still, but she'd been disoriented and in pain. And nauseous. She remembered all too well throwing up when they'd transferred her from the gurney to the examining table.

"Lousy patient," she'd heard someone say, but in a teasing voice. Jenny Blackwell. No more sharing her gourmet coffee stash with Jenny.

"Was it Billy Long?" she asked now. She seemed to have a vague memory of someone asking her that.

"We think so," Luke said, adding with disgust, "although no one saw anything, including you."

"Because the security light was out," Keely told him. She remembered noticing it after she got

Matthew into the car. "Are you sure Matthew's okay with Randall?"

"He's fine." Luke jiggled the line feeding her IV, then tapped it to improve the flow.

"What's he doing? Baby-sitting in his office until I can drive Matthew home?"

Luke leaned against her bed, as handsome and sexy as a movie star in his white lab coat. It was easy to see why half the nurses lusted after him. "That's hardly a workable suggestion, Keely. Just think about it. You won't be driving for a couple of days, because you'll be right here."

"*That's* the unworkable suggestion, Luke. I can't hang around here. Matthew needs me. Just because I got a little roughed up—"

"A *little* roughed up? You were out fifteen minutes."

"In and out," she argued. "Not totally unconscious."

"What about your bruised kidneys? And your thigh looks like you've been kickboxing. Plus you've got multiple scrapes and cuts, not to mention a nasty finger sprain."

For the first time, she noticed the bandage on her left hand as Luke lifted it up for her to see. "How did that happen?"

"Defensive injury."

"Oh. Yeah." Now she remembered trying to fend off her attacker as he'd smacked her in the face. Fat chance. The man had been wild with rage. "I wish now I'd let you take Matthew home. This wouldn't have happened."

"Matthew needed some TLC after getting those stitches. You did the right thing."

"I just hope he didn't see anything."

"I don't think he did, but he knew you were hurt."

Now he was sitting on the edge of her bed. "What if Laura's mean to him?"

"To Matthew?" He was shaking his head, smiling. "That's morphine talking, Keely. I promise you, she would never be unkind to a child."

She wasn't so sure, but was in no shape to argue. Fighting a yawn, she struggled to stay awake, but was unable to resist the pleasure of Luke's touch when he cupped her cheek.

"Randall told me she's had a change of heart," he said, brushing his thumb over her lips.

"Maybe where Matthew's concerned," Keely murmured, snuggling dreamily into the warmth of his palm. "That doesn't include me."

"You don't know that."

She thought of the conversation with her father and felt tears welling in her eyes. The morphine was making her weepy. She looked at Luke. "I told Randall everything, did you know that?"

"You mentioned it."

"I did? When?"

"When you were lying on the sidewalk with about twenty people hovering above you, Randall included."

Imagining the worst, she tried to frown but found it was just too much trouble. "What did I say?"

"We'll talk about it tomorrow."

She was entering a soft, cushiony twilight zone, but she fumbled for his hand, giving it a shake. "No, I want to know now."

He turned her palm up and kissed it. "You were disoriented and in pain. Randall was as frantic as...well, as any father would be. You seemed to sense his concern."

"I don't...remember...any of that."

Luke smiled wryly. "That's okay, there'll be at least half a dozen folks eager to refresh your memory."

"What...did I say, Luke? Please."

"You said—and this is a direct quote—'Don't worry, Dad, I won't tell anybody our secret.'"

IN THE MORNING, she awoke to find Detective Evans standing by her bed. Her room was a small private one and his massive body clad in yet another thick down vest seemed to fill every inch of available space. She could easily imagine how he must intimidate suspects who had the misfortune to come under suspicion by him. Luke, she noticed, was stationed on the other side of her bed.

She lifted a hand and let it fall limply. "Detective Evans, long time no see."

"Maybe—" the detective smiled "—if you don't count last night."

"You were here last night?" So *that's* where that vague notion came from that she'd answered some questions about Billy Long.

"I warned you she might not remember," Luke told him.

Evans shrugged. "No problem, I'm used to going over the testimony of victims."

"You get a lot of victims, do you?" Luke asked, heavy on the sarcasm. He obviously hadn't forgotten that Evans had refused police protection for Keely.

"I get my share," Evans said laconically. He pulled out a small black notebook. "Now...if you feel like it, Dr. Hamilton, I'd like—"

"After I check her," Luke said curtly, grabbing her chart.

"No problem," Evans murmured, and turned to leave. "I'll just step outside. Yell when you're ready."

"Wait a minute," Keely said, halting the detective at the door. "I'm okay, Luke. I can answer a few questions without having a relapse."

"You've suffered severe trauma, Keely. I've

known other patients to unravel over something like this.''

''Wimps,'' she joked. ''And I'm not one.''

Luke moved closer and, before she could object, pulled a penlight from his jacket pocket. He clicked it on. ''Just checking your pupils,'' he murmured in a low tone, very close to her face.

Keely let him do it, and asked in the same low tone, ''Is there any change from the last time you checked—'' she paused ''—at three this morning?''

He'd stayed with her all night in spite of her insisting it wasn't necessary. Several times she'd come partially awake when he got up to check on her. She thought she remembered turning and finding herself in his arms. But that had to have been a dream induced by morphine. As a resident, he would have earned a severe reprimand, had anybody walked in. And because she, too, was also on staff, a reprimand would have been just for starters. Such behavior could wreck a career. She knew Luke wouldn't allow anything to jeopardize his career. Only drugs could have produced such a fantasy.

Luke clicked off the tiny light and tucked it into his pocket. ''Looks good.'' Then, with his back to Detective Evans, he ran his finger along her lips. ''Feels good, too,'' he murmured, for her ears alone.

She drew in a sharp breath and would have moaned, except for the presence of Detective Evans, who chose that moment to speak.

"Maybe I should leave you two alone."

"No!" Keely said. "I'm ready. To answer your questions," she added hastily.

Making a great show of it, Evans again pulled his notebook out of his pocket and clicked the point on his pen, prepared to write. "Did you recognize your assailant, Dr. Hamilton?"

She gave him a surprised look. "It was Billy Long, wasn't it?"

"That's what you're supposed to tell me. You're the one who was attacked."

She glanced at Luke. "Well, I mean…I *think* it was Billy Long. I've only seen him in person one time—here at the hospital the night we treated Phyllis. But it was dark last night. The security light wasn't working."

"Probably thanks to your guy," Evans said. "But did you see his face?"

"I couldn't." She struggled to get up on one elbow, looking at him eagerly. "I mean, it would have been impossible even if the light had been working. He wore a stocking over his face! I just remembered that."

Luke gave her a gentle nudge, forcing her to settle back on the pillows. "If you insist on bouncing around, then let me roll your bed up some."

"Anything else, Dr. Hamilton?" The detective was looking at her. So far, he hadn't written anything down.

Keely frowned, thinking as Luke took the remote to raise the head of her bed. "He said something."

"You didn't mention that when I questioned you last night."

"I don't even remember talking to you last night, Detective Evans."

"Surprise, surprise," Luke said softly.

But the words her attacker said as he cursed her were coming back now. "He was in a rage. It was like he wanted to kill me, he was so mad. And it was *me* he was mad at."

"What makes you say that?" Evans asked.

She shuddered, remembering. "He said I'd killed his wife."

"Why would he say that?" Evans asked.

"I'm just guessing," Luke said, "but he probably thinks Keely was responsible for Phyllis taking off because Keely agreed to look after Matthew. Of course, he conveniently overlooks the fact that he killed her once he found her."

Evans grunted. "Anything else?"

"I don't think so." Keely frowned, then shook her head. "No, that's all he said."

Evans was on his feet now. "And did you or did you not recognize the voice as Billy Long's?"

She gave a shrug. "Well, who else could it be?"

Luke faced Evans across Keely's bed. "She was almost killed by that maniac, Evans. Is it possible *now* to assign her some police protection?"

"I don't think it'll be necessary, Dr. Jamison." Evans flipped the cover on his notebook and tucked it into his shirt pocket beneath his thick vest. "We picked Billy Long up last night. He's in custody downtown being held on suspicion-of-murder charges."

"Well, hell!" Luke exploded. "Why didn't you say so?"

"I'm saying so now." Evans stood up. "Long denies everything, naturally. They all do. But I think you can rest easy for a while." He went to the door and opened it, giving them a courteous farewell nod. "Both of you."

KEELY LAY THINKING after Luke and Detective Evans left. She knew what she had to do. With Billy Long in jail, there was no reason for Luke to be with her every minute she wasn't at the hospital. It was possible he might still be willing to help her with Matthew—she hoped he would—but if he refused, she would simply manage. She wasn't the only single woman who was forced to think creatively for the sake of a child. And she would tell Luke that as soon as she got out of here.

CHAPTER FOURTEEN

LUKE HEADED for Keely's room the next morning in a black mood. She'd agreed to spend another night in the hospital, but hadn't let him stay with her again. Consequently, he'd spent a restless night alone, missing her like hell. With a brief knock, he pushed her door open and found her packing to leave.

"Don't start, Luke. I'm fine. I'm a little achy and I'm favoring that bruised thigh when I walk, but I can convalesce just as well at my own apartment as here."

Grabbing her chart, Luke scowled at it before scribbling something down. His frustration was mixed with a strange urgency. He liked being in control, but that wasn't going to happen with Keely. "I'm just surprised you allowed yourself thirty-six hours to overcome a brutal attack," he replied. "But if you insist on checking out, it's your funeral."

"I'll be taking a few days off," she said, dumping toothbrush and toiletries into a gym bag and ignoring the funeral remark. "Lawrence insisted."

Lawrence Waldrop was the hospital administrator. Luke guessed the time off had nothing to do with any concern on Waldrop's part regarding Keely's well-being. Since the attack had taken place on hospital grounds, he was afraid she might sue. He was a weak-kneed ass.

"How many days off?" Luke asked, still holding the chart.

"A week."

"Sounds good. I'm finishing up my E.R. rotation, then I'm scheduled for Oncology. But I'll have a few days off, too. It couldn't work out better." He slipped the pen back into his pocket. "How does a trip to New Orleans sound? You persuaded your mother not to come up, but if she's like most mothers, I bet she'd like to see for herself that you're okay."

"I don't think so."

"You don't think your mother would like to see you?"

She reached for a book on the bedside table and threw it into the gym bag. "No, I meant I don't think it's a good idea for us to go to New Orleans."

A keen look at her face told him everything. It wasn't that she didn't want to go to New Orleans, or see her mother. She just didn't want him tagging along. He was unprepared for the violence of the emotion that washed through him—shock, disbelief, a fierce need to change her mind. And fear that he couldn't. But he pulled himself together. Being blindsided was nothing new. He'd had plenty of experience as a kid enduring setbacks. And pain. He just hadn't expected it from Keely.

"What about Matthew?" he asked, watching her take a jacket from the metal locker.

"I'm on my way to get him right now."

"Are you sure you're up to it? According to Randall, Matthew and Laura are getting along just fine. He could probably stay another day or so...until you feel a little stronger." Luke was thinking a couple of days alone, they might get beyond this.

"I'm strong enough now," Keely said, zipping up the gym bag. "And Matthew doesn't belong there. He belongs with me." She set the bag on her bed and looked at her watch. "I told Randall to expect me at his house at nine o'clock."

He was watching her intently. "He's 'Randall' now, not 'Dad'?"

She snapped her fingers. "My slippers..." She disappeared into the bathroom to get them. "That was a slip of the tongue and I regret it."

"You were in a state of shock, Keely."

"Yes...well, intimacies like that can come later. First, we probably need to get used to the idea of...you know...being related."

He studied her in silence, trying to ignore the

knot settling in his stomach. This was about Billy
Long, he thought. Now that the cops had him in
custody and booked for Phyllis's murder, the threat
to Keely was essentially over. She had no need for
protection. And with Laura willing to step into the
breach and help her care for Matthew, Luke was
suddenly reading the handwriting on the wall.

He looked at her face, bruised but beautiful. Her
mouth—he could almost taste it!—was soft, kiss-
able. She'd tucked her tawny hair behind one ear
and revealed the delicate line of her throat. He
knew the taste of her there, too, as well as every
other inch of her. He could see the outline of her
braless breasts in the big shirt she wore, and had
to work to keep from touching her. Once he did,
his hands would take on a life of their own, roam-
ing all over her, lingering, caressing, claiming.
Goddamn it! And she thought she'd just walk
away?

"Okay," he said, driving a hand through his
hair. "I know I did some…damage to our relationship a couple of days ago when you brought
up the subject of marriage."

She stopped with a furious look, still holding the
slippers. "You make it sound as if I was fishing
for a proposal! I was speaking hypothetically,
damn it. I still believe Matthew needs a mother and
a father and I'm going to be extremely particular
about who that is." She crammed the slippers in-

side the bag and zipped it up again. "And don't worry, I don't have you in my sights."

"Look, Keely…" He could lose her, he realized with real fear. "I only meant that marriage hadn't been something I'd thought of before you…before it was mentioned. It caught me off guard."

"Well, now you can relax."

"No! You don't understand." He looked at her, his tongue tied in a knot, wrestling with a hundred emotions. He thought of trying to explain about his own lousy father, about his fear that he'd make the same mistakes. He thought of telling her about the boy in Bosnia. But after too many years of bottling up feelings, the words were locked in his throat.

"Actually—" Keely sat back down on the bed "—you were correct in seeing that marriage was a bad idea. For us. Even if the thought briefly came to mind. We really don't know each other that well. Working together for a six-week E.R. rotation wasn't enough time for us to get to know each other. And we both know too many married couples who've split up before their residency ended. It was an unusual set of circumstances that threw us together to begin with. Now that's finished. It's not as if there's some urgent reason for us to resort to marriage. You were right."

"Resort to marriage?"

She waved a hand, not looking at him. "You know what I mean."

"Yeah, I think I do. I think you don't need my help anymore, so I'm being dumped."

"You're the one who said we should just continue along as we were, Luke. I'm agreeing with that, for the time being."

"You didn't seem to like that idea when I said it a few days ago."

"Temporary insanity," she said. "This whole thing has been…well, as I said, unusual. My God, it started with a woman's murder. The circumstances were…are extraordinary. We just have to tolerate each other for a few more days until I figure out what to do—for Matthew's sake."

"We can get married." He blurted it out in frustration. But the moment he said it, Luke knew that was exactly what they should do. Something that had been in turmoil deep inside him eased. He felt a sense of calm. It was the same reaction he'd had when he'd made the decision to leave the Army and enter med school. When something was right, it was right.

She smiled, but it wasn't pretty. "I'm really not that desperate, Luke."

"You're saying no?"

Taking a deep breath, she stood up. "Could you drive me back to my place to get my car?"

He'd have to find a way to persuade her. Hell, did she think he'd just let her go, let her take Matthew after he'd learned to love him? Did she think he'd just disappear? In her dreams!

He glanced at her bandaged left hand. "You're going to try to drive and manage a four-year-old with one hand?"

She lifted the gym bag. "That's the plan."

Before she had a chance to object, he took it from her, gripped her elbow with his other hand and ushered her out of the room. She might not need him in her bed or as a protector or as a husband, but she wasn't getting out of his sight until he'd had a chance to try to fix things.

"Meeting Laura could be awkward," he said. "You may be glad to have me along once the two of you are face-to-face." He opened the door and waited for her to go ahead of him. "Or maybe she doesn't know yet."

"She knows. Randall said he told her everything."

"How did she take it?"

"He said she's…working on it. Which is fine with me." She waited for a patient who was tethered to a rolling IV pole to shuffle past them. "I can understand she's shocked, probably scandalized. Discovering her husband has an illegitimate child has to be about the last thing a minister's wife would expect."

"You assume she's going to resent you. That might not happen."

"Actually, I thought what Randall said was pretty revealing. I mean, if she was happy, he'd have said so, wouldn't he? I'm sure she wishes I'd stayed a deep, dark secret in his past, but he's too nice to tell me that."

He walked beside her toward the elevators, slowing his pace to match hers. "Seems to me it might be more logical to punish Randall, not you."

She pushed the down button and waited for the elevator. "Luke, I didn't want anybody punished."

IT WAS LAURA, not Randall, who opened the door when they rang the bell. She invited them inside, her expression so polite that they might have been complete strangers. Keely was almost amused at the extreme contrast in her manner and the welcoming interior of her house.

"Matthew's in the kitchen decorating cookies," Laura said, turning to lead them to him.

"Wait…" Keely touched Luke's arm. "Will you go to Matthew and keep him occupied for a few minutes? I want to talk to your aunt alone. If he sees me, he won't want to wait for us to finish our grown-up talk. Please."

When Luke left them, Laura said to Keely with more excruciating politeness, "We can talk in the living room."

"Thanks." Keely entered the beautifully formal room through the arched entrance. It was the same place they'd talked before, but this time there was no huge flower arrangement on the coffee table to serve as a barrier between them. Candles in every shape and size were placed here and there in holders that were unique and, Keely guessed, carefully chosen. The woman truly had exquisite taste. Keely could only imagine what Laura would think of her place, with its comfortable but mostly secondhand furnishings.

"I hope you're recovering from the...attack," Laura said. "Will there be any lingering effects?"

"There shouldn't be, no." Keely held up her hand. "This is just a finger sprain and it'll be awkward trying to work until it heals. I'm taking a few days off."

"You were lucky."

"I was. Actually, it was Randall who happened along, which probably saved me. Did you know that?"

"Yes, he told me." Laura looked at a collection of photos—to Keely, a treasure trove of family likenesses—arranged on a baby grand piano. "He was very upset."

"Mrs. Barlow—"

Laura drew a deep breath. "He also told me that night who you really are."

Keely prayed to find the right words to begin building a relationship with this woman. Otherwise, she might never get to know her father except in a very general sense.

"I'm glad to have this opportunity to tell you that I regret any shock or unhappiness you might feel about discovering my...connection to Randall."

"It was certainly a shock."

Keely leaned forward to make her point. "You probably can't understand how important it was to me to try and find my father. I've known his identity for several years, but when I got here I decided not to say anything. He had a lovely wife, the respect of everyone who knew him, a spotless reputation. He made me proud to think that I might have some of his traits. The truth is, I simply allowed myself to enjoy being around him, working with him. I certainly didn't want to be the cause of any more strife in his family."

"You mean after Shelley died."

"Yes." Keely examined the bandage on her hand. "I can only imagine your pain. I couldn't say anything then, could I?" Laura was silent. "But when you began to misinterpret things, I felt I had to say something."

"I feel foolish now," Laura said, "under the circumstances."

"You shouldn't. How could you have known?"

"I jumped to a hysterical conclusion," Laura said, but the words were spoken without rancor.

"A very human reaction," Keely said gently. "Anyone can make a mistake when they don't know all the facts. I've certainly made a few." Unable to resist, she glanced at the piano. "Are those pictures on the piano of Randall's family?"

"And mine, yes." Laura's gaze roamed over the collection. "I suppose you're curious."

"I don't have many relatives," Keely explained.

"You have your mother."

"And she's a twin. My aunt Stephanie has children, so I've got three cousins. But that's it."

"Randall's parents are deceased."

"Oh." So she had no grandparents. She felt a little pang of disappointment.

"You look like his mother."

"Really?"

Laura got up and took a framed portrait from the piano and gave it to Keely, who stared in fascination. "She was very beautiful. I always hoped Randall wouldn't compare me with his mother. I'd come up hopelessly lacking."

To Keely's surprise, she thought she detected a little humor in Laura's remark. "You're different types," Keely said, fascinated at this intimate glimpse of the woman who was, in reality, her stepmother. "But just as lovely. People tell me I look a lot like my mother."

"Perhaps. But you're so much like Shelley that—" Her voice broke. "You want to hear something strange? I think now that I saw that resemblance from the moment I met you, but I put it out of my mind. Which probably explains why I concocted excuses to avoid being around you. I think Randall saw the same thing, but he reacted just the opposite. He was drawn to you, instead."

Keely could only stare. "That's...I don't know what to say, Mrs. Barlow."

"Shouldn't you call me Laura?" There was a wry tone in her voice. "Formal address between us seems a little silly, doesn't it?"

Keely nodded. "I suppose so."

"As for pain, I'll be honest and tell you that since Randall shared this secret from his past, I've been a basket case. I've felt so many emotions in the past two days that I hardly know which end is up." Her hands moved restlessly in her lap. "This will make me sound so petty and small and mean-spirited, but Randall says feelings just *are* and I can't help what I feel. My first thought was the injustice of it all. Why should he find a long-lost daughter to fill the emptiness left with Shelley's death when there's no chance of that ever happening for me?" Tears in her eyes, she looked into Keely's face. "Isn't that awful?"

"I think it's like Randall says," Keely said gently, "feelings just are. And I can never replace Shelley in your husband's heart, Laura. Never in a million years. I wouldn't want to."

"Yes, well—" She'd found a tissue and delicately blew her nose. "You've always been special to him. I know he noticed the resemblance, too."

"Maybe it's something you two could talk about."

"I really wish we could." She sniffed and blotted the corners of her eyes. "It's funny, they say men are the ones who find it hard to express feelings. But Randall's not like that. So many times I wanted to tell him what I was feeling about you. I wanted to share the strange…empathy that was present the few times I saw you. But I let other feelings get in the way."

Keely smiled. "You sound a lot like my mother. She's all bottled up, too. I must have inherited that gene from my father. I blab everything I think."

Now Laura managed a smile. "It's a good gene. Be glad it's in the family."

Keely's smile faded. "Your nephew certainly doesn't have it."

"Luke?"

"Yes. He's as…as closemouthed and unreadable as a sphinx."

"His father was a tyrant, did you know that? Luke learned early not to show his feelings." She rose and took down another photograph from the collection on the piano. "This is his mother—my sister—and Robert, his father. It was taken about twenty years ago. He was a handsome devil, wasn't he? *Devil* being the operative word.''

''Yes.'' And Luke looked incredibly like him.

''They look alike,'' Laura said, guessing Keely's thoughts. ''But Luke is ten times the man his father was. He's honorable and sensitive and decent, more like Randall than Robert Jamison. You're lucky to have the love of a man like Luke.''

Keely was startled. Luke loved her? ''I don't think—I mean, Luke and I haven't—'' She stopped, took a breath. ''What I mean to say is that our relationship isn't what it seems. We had to do something about Matthew and—''

Laura reached out and patted her knee. ''You mean that, since it was Matthew who brought you together, that only concern for his welfare keeps you together?''

''I— Yes. We're just friends.''

''Well, of course I could be wrong,'' she said, and smiled, ''but when you were attacked he certainly didn't react as a friend would. From what Randall said he was like a wild man. I drew my own conclusions when he came here to check on Matthew and all he could talk about was you, your injuries, how vulnerable you were, how he'd like to get his hands on Billy Long.'' She stood up and spoke briskly. ''Speaking of Matthew, I think I hear him coming.''

Still stiff and sore, Keely didn't have time to get

up. Yelling joyously, Matthew was already barreling into the living room and diving into her arms. "Keely, Keely! You came back, you came back! I knew you would. Auntie Laura said you would."

Ignoring her painful bruises, Keely wrapped her arms around Matthew and hugged him with all her might. Resting her cheek against the top of his towhead, she breathed in the little-boy smell of him—cookies and sweat and dog. Oscar was with him, tail wagging, tongue lolling in a doggie grin. He greeted Keely with a deep woof. She laughed and dodged the big Lab's efforts to lick her face.

Luke caught him by the collar. "See," he said, "Oz still loves you."

"I love you, too, Keely," said Matthew, his small arms tight around her neck. Then he settled himself beside her, content for once to snuggle and be snuggled. She curled her arm around him, thanking God that her father had come along in time to keep Billy Long from hurting Matthew.

"I missed you, honey bun," she said, dropping a kiss on the top of his head.

He looked up into her face anxiously. "I thought Luke was going to protect us, Keely. He wasn't going to let Billy hurt anybody anymore."

"Billy won't hurt anybody ever again," she told him. "The police have him locked up in jail."

Matthew was nodding enthusiastically. "Good. I'm glad." He scrambled off the couch and took her hand, urging her to her feet. "Now, let's go home!"

STAYING WITH THE BARLOWS WAS, of course, never an option. On the way home, Luke and Keely had discussed, and rejected, the possibility of Matthew being anywhere except with them. In this one thing, at least, both were in agreement. There would still be some juggling of their schedules until something permanent could be worked out, but for the next few days both would try not to let the uncertainty of Matthew's future ruin Christmas for him, or for them.

Tomorrow was Christmas Eve. Having time off around Christmas and New Year's was a minor miracle, and Keely wasn't going to question a miracle, even when she'd had to have been mugged by Billy Long to inspire it. Keely was undecided about going to New Orleans. Her mother would dearly love to see her and was openly curious about Matthew. Which was understandable since Keely's phone conversations had been filled with Matthew anecdotes for weeks. Her eyes rested on Luke's hands on the wheel. She admitted it wasn't fair to Luke to skip off to New Orleans and deprive him of Christmas morning with Matthew. He'd bought as many gifts for the little boy as Keely. Maybe more…and he was sure to bring up the subject of the trip again.

Once they got home, Luke went inside with them, as always. While Matthew went to his room to check that everything was as he'd left it—Elmo on his pillow, a snowy Christmas scene under a glass bubble on his bedside table and his bucket of Lego inside his closet—Keely checked her voice mail. There was nothing unusual except a message from Detective Evans. When Luke checked his messages, he had one, too. Even with Billy Long in jail, she still felt a little uneasy. One advantage of spending Christmas in New Orleans was knowing there was several hundred miles between them and that crazy man.

She dialed Evans's number and the detective answered on the first ring. "Hey, Doc. They told me you'd escaped from St. Dominic's, but I didn't believe it. How'd you get Jamison to spring you so quick? He had me thinking you'd be in there a couple more days."

"I told them I wasn't up to any more interrogations by the cops."

"Hmm, whatever works, eh?"

Beside her, Luke was looking impatient and wanting her to get on with it. "You left a message for me to call?" she prodded.

"Yeah. I don't know whether this is good news or bad, but we've identified Raymond Tucker."

"Who?"

"Raymond Tucker. Did I forget to mention we

finally uncovered the name of the kid's father? Turned up in some papers left behind by Phyllis Long—her divorce decree.''

''No, you didn't mention that,'' Keely said, feeling her heart constricting with shock. And dread. Matthew's father was alive?

Luke must have heard her distress. ''What's the matter?'' he demanded.

She turned away as Evans was still talking. ''I don't know much about him, but he doesn't sound much like a doting parent and, to tell the truth, I suspect we'll find he isn't interested in a four-year-old kid. He's got a record, served three years for petty stuff—bad checks, embezzlement at the garage where he worked and possession.''

''Possession?''

''Yeah, cocaine. It was his second offense and it was enough to send him away.''

''Oh, no. But surely they wouldn't let a man like that have custody of a child.'' But they would. Didn't she have firsthand knowledge of just how blind the system could be? If the case landed in the hands of an overworked, burnt-out bureaucrat, anything could happen.

''Who, not Matthew?'' Luke was trying to get her attention again. ''What's he saying about custody?''

She covered the receiver. ''They've learned who

Matthew's father is.'' Unaware of the distress he was creating, Evans continued to fill her in.

''Well, you know the law usually weighs in on the side of a parent in these cases, Doc, and if he *should* show some interest…''

''No,'' she said sharply. ''I won't let them do it.''

Evans made a sympathetic sound. ''You can always fight it, but I gotta tell you, if the man's kept out of trouble and seems stable, his claim will carry some weight.''

''And does he?''

''Seem stable? Well, his parole officer says he hasn't seen him for a few weeks, but it's Christmas and he eases up a little on the rules during the holidays. He tells me Tucker has a job—or at least he did last time the P.O. checked. That's a plus for him. We're in the process of trying to locate him, which is why I called. I knew you and Dr. Jamison would be interested.''

Interested!

''When he turns up,'' Evans was saying, ''we'll have to give him a chance to take the boy. That is, *if* he wants him.''

''Matthew's never mentioned any other man except Billy Long being in his life,'' Keely said, her voice rising with panic. ''He can't be given to a stranger. This man could be violent. He could have a drug problem. At the very least, he's been out of Matthew's life for years!''

"I understand your concern, Doc. Sometimes the law doesn't make a lot of sense. I'd go to the wire to prevent Tucker from taking him if it comes to that, I give you my word. But I felt you should know the lay of the land and be prepared.''

She hung up and stared blankly at the phone. "I won't let them do it,'' she said again. Inside, she felt the urge to throw some things in a bag, grab Matthew and flee.

Luke caught her arms and gave her a little shake. "What did he say? Where in hell is this guy? Where's he been?''

"In prison.''

"Good Lord.''

She told him everything.

CHAPTER FIFTEEN

KEELY WAS FORCED TO take it easy for the rest of that day, but by midafternoon, she insisted they go Christmas shopping. Matthew wanted to buy gifts for Luke and Keely. It was a bittersweet moment for her. To others, they must have seemed like a real family—Mom, Dad and little boy. To Matthew, too. When Luke left, it was going to be difficult to explain why.

That night, Luke grilled two steaks while she gave Matthew his bath and put him to bed. He was asleep in minutes, his arm curled around his friend Elmo. Shelley Barlow's brown teddy bear was propped on the bedside table beside Matthew's Christmas snow scene. Later Keely would sit down and think about her amazing talk with Laura Barlow, but not just now. Raymond Tucker and what, if anything, he might do about Matthew had pushed all other considerations from her mind.

Don't worry, Matthew, I won't let them hand you over to some loser you don't even know, biological father or not.

Matthew didn't deserve having his world turned

upside down again. The little boy mentioned his mother less and less now. In a way, it saddened Keely, but she hoped it meant he was coming to accept the fact that Phyllis was never returning. It was clear to everyone that Keely and Luke had replaced his mother and whatever fatherly role Billy Long had played in his world.

All of which made Keely's dilemma even more distressful. People didn't just get married for the sake of a child, no matter how much they both loved him. When a relationship soured and ended in divorce, it was the children who suffered the most. And considering Luke's reluctance to make a heartfelt commitment, a split was almost inevitable down the line.

Murmuring a good-night, Keely brushed Matthew's hair from his cheek and kissed him. Oscar, curled up at the foot of the bed, thumped his tail twice and settled down for the night. When she turned, Luke was standing in the doorway watching her. In one hand, he held a metal spatula, in the other a bottle of wine.

"The steaks are ready," he said. Tough-looking and sexy in a dark sweatshirt and jeans, he was more mouthwatering than any sizzling steak. "Are you hungry?"

"Starving," she said brightly. Moving past him, she headed for the kitchen. "I'll set the table."

"No need." He tossed the spatula into the sink

and ushered her into the dining area where the table was set with candles, cloth napkins and wineglasses that sparkled in the soft flames. He pulled out her chair, waited for her to sit, then poured wine for both of them.

She took the glass he handed her. "You accomplished all this while I was bathing Matthew?"

"Steaks are quick," he said with a shrug. "It takes ten minutes to nuke two potatoes and I'm very fast at chopping green stuff." He sat down and held up his glass. "Let's toast."

"To what?" she asked warily. She'd fallen into bed with him all too easily. She wasn't going to let herself be seduced as effortlessly by his domestic skills. Or his thoughtfulness in fixing dinner while she fussed over Matthew. Of all people, Luke knew how upset she was to learn about Raymond Tucker.

"To us."

She set the glass down. "Did you hear anything I said in that hospital room, Luke?"

"I heard everything. So what does that have to do with a simple toast to us? It's only you and me here, so I'd hardly toast anybody else, would I?"

"You know what I mean." She gestured at the table, the food, all the elements for a seduction. "This may be the way you've resolved differences with other women, but it's not going to work with me. We've said what needs to be said. We understand where each of us is coming from now.''

"I've never cared enough about another woman to light candles and use fancy napkins,'' he told her. Then he pushed his chair back and stood up. "And we haven't said all that needs to be said, Keely. I do understand where you're coming from, but you're in the dark about me and what I think.''

"Well, if that's so, whose fault is it?''

"I was sincere when I proposed, damn it!''

"You were sincere when you panicked the night before when *I* proposed!'' she retorted. "Which I've already admitted was a bad idea.''

"It was *not* a bad idea! It was the *right* idea.'' He almost growled with frustration. "Look, I made a mistake, okay? I've admitted it. Now, let's just forget all that and start planning to get married and—''

"And what'll happen if Raymond Tucker shows up and takes Matthew? Is that contingency in your plan?''

His frown grew even darker. "That won't happen.''

"You can't possibly know that!''

"We can fight it. Matthew's best interest is not served by turning him over to some ex-con, that's just common sense. He's clearly happy and thriving here with us, even though it's only a few weeks since his mother died. And if we're married, that will make our case to keep him even stronger.''

Her appetite gone, Keely rose from the table, wincing a little from her bruised ribs. She sat down gingerly on the couch. ''You haven't experienced the system from the inside as I have,'' she said. Leaning back, she studied the angel on the top of her Christmas tree. ''They're perfectly capable of doing something as crazy as handing Matthew over to his biological father, ex-con or not. If Tucker is employed, if he tests drug-free and if he wants Matthew, he'll get him. That a married couple is standing by begging for him won't matter one iota in a court of law with a judge who has an idea that blood parents are the best parents. If that judge decides Tucker is rehabilitated, he'll get to keep his son.''

''And I say you're making assumptions based on your own hang-ups. There was no one looking out for your interests when you were a kid, Keely. You and I are willing to do anything for Matthew. That'll make a difference to the court, to any judge with a smattering of sensitivity.''

''And I say *you're* making assumptions based on ignorance of the system. You've only seen it from the outside looking in, Luke. I've been there and done it.''

He sat down on the couch beside her. ''Then I

say we wait and see. But getting married is a good first step.''

''No, it isn't. We'd be marrying for the wrong reasons.'' She could feel the tension shimmering off Luke, but she wasn't going to be pushed into marriage. She loved him and, until he loved her, it would be a betrayal of everything she believed in to marry for any other reason.

She thought of her mother and Daniel and the depth of their love for each other. Aunt Stephanie and Uncle Tal shared the same thing. You couldn't be around them thirty seconds without seeing they were crazy about each other. She wanted that and nothing less when she got married. All the love on one side spelled doom for any marriage.

''We'll fight for Matthew,'' she told Luke, ''but we won't get married for his sake.''

''This is getting us nowhere, damn it!'' He surprised her by reaching out and curling his hand around her neck to pull her close. Before she could react, he was kissing her. She made a little sound, but it died with the first taste of him. There was desperation in his kiss. The tension she'd sensed in him a minute before turned into a wholly male compulsion to urge her surrender. She knew what he was doing. She knew how he intended this to end, but in spite of all the reasons she shouldn't, her arms went around him. She would allow herself another moment, one more nanosecond only of pleasure.

Careful of her injuries, he laid her down on the couch and then his hands were all over her, shaping her breasts, squeezing her buttocks, seeking the softness of her inner thigh. And she was kissing him back with the same frantic hunger. While his mouth swallowed her strangled breaths, he was pulling at her clothes, pushing her top up, and breaking the kiss only enough to remove the sweater and toss it aside. Then, some caution stirred again in Keely, reminding her that this wasn't going to solve their problems, but she was distracted by his hand slipping beneath the waistband of her jeans before she could do anything.

His passion was contagious. Heat rose in her, flushing her face, constricting muscles deep inside her.

Luke was breathing right in her ear as she rocked mindlessly toward a climax. "I need you, too, sweetheart," he murmured, and withdrew his hand.

She whimpered, coming back to earth with a shock. Luke was lifting up a bit to get at the button on his jeans. The pause was enough to let reason flood back.

"Wait, Luke," she said, putting out a hand. "This is not the way to fix things."

For a moment, Luke continued to work at his

zipper, then he looked at her. Tears glistened in her eyes. Her mouth trembled. Realization of what he was doing slammed into him, followed by a wave of shame that felt like a tidal wave.

Damn! There was a name for what he'd almost done.

He rubbed a hand over his face, unable to look at her. "I'm sorry," he said, almost choking on the words. "I— You must think—"

"I think we both got carried away." But there was a bleak look in her eyes.

Feeling shocked himself at how out of control he'd been, he helped her sit up. Then he got to his feet, moving slowly, weighted down by regret. Finally he found the courage to meet her eyes. She was staring at him, half-naked, still breathing fast, the bruises from Billy Long's attack clearly visible in all their ugly reality. She looked like a victim of abuse. And he was the abuser!

"You may not believe this, but I've never done anything like that before, Keely."

"It's…okay," she said breathlessly. "I shouldn't have let it go so far. I… It just felt…so good."

"Yeah, it felt good." *Too good.*

"I've never denied the sexual attraction between us."

"I need to go." He looked around blankly for his jacket, intent only on getting to the door. Spotting it, he swept it up from a chair nearby, not bothering to put it on.

Keely hurriedly grabbed a knitted throw from the couch and wrapped it around herself to follow him. "I'd like to talk about this, Luke."

"Later, okay? Not now." He had the door open and was gulping in drafts of cold, crisp night air. He was shaken. The capacity for brutality was buried deep in him, a legacy from his father; he'd always known that. But he'd never come close to falling into the abyss. He was a healer, a physician. How had this happened? Was he truly like his father? Resorting to force whenever he was frustrated or angry?

Keely tugged the throw up over her shoulder. "Do you realize what you were doing? Your arguments couldn't persuade me so you thought you'd soften me up with some steamy sex. That you'd even try something like that should tell you how doomed a marriage between us would be."

"I said I was sorry."

He felt her studying his profile as he stared into the night. Everywhere he looked, Christmas lights glowed, outside houses, inside windows, on rooftops. It had begun to snow softly. Tomorrow— Christmas Eve—Matthew would wake to an all-white world. He would be ecstatic.

Keely sighed and her tone eased. "I like making love with you, Luke. But I'm going to need more than good sex and polite conversation when I marry. I want to love and *be* loved. But more importantly, I'm going to want the man who loves me to *talk!*''

He turned now and his gaze was dark, unreadable. "Lock the door when I leave, okay?"

KEELY STOOD DRAPED in the fuzzy throw for a long moment before reaching to turn the dead bolt and snap off the light in the foyer. Moving to the window, she watched Luke make his way across the street, the collar of his jacket turned up and his shoulders hunched against the swirling snow. In a few moments, he reached his own apartment and went inside.

With a sigh, she went back to the living room and as she bent to pick up her sweater from the floor, she thought she heard a small noise. Was Matthew awake? Oh, Lord, she hoped he hadn't heard that. All he'd ever known from the people closest to him was discord and strife. He'd been spared that while he'd been cared for by her and Luke. At least, until tonight.

Then, as she was pulling the sweater on over her head, Oscar suddenly burst into furious barking. She froze in alarm, instantly thinking of an intruder. Then she realized that was ridiculous. They'd beefed up security. She had new locks, and

Billy Long was in jail. Matthew must be teasing him, or else he heard something outside.

Hurrying past the table, she noted vaguely the candles still flickering, mute evidence of the aborted dinner. "Oscar! Be quiet!"

But the big dog's bark was more frantic than ever. There was a strange sound and a sharp, short yelp from Oscar. Then Matthew screamed. Her heart stopped. Oh, God, someone was in the house! Thinking only to get to Matthew, she dashed down the hall just in time to see a man lift Oscar by the collar and hurl him bodily into a closet.

She flew to the bed, reaching for Matthew, who threw his small arms around her and buried his face in her middle. *Oh, God, no. Don't let him be hurt again. Please, please, please.*

She turned her own terrified gaze on the man, who held a baseball bat and was bumping it against one thick thigh. He was a hulking brute of a man, well over six feet. His face was totally unfamiliar.

"What do you want?" Keely managed, clutching Matthew, whose trembling body echoed her own terror. "Who are you?"

She stared at him, trying to match her vague memory of Billy Long with this man, but it wouldn't compute in her brain. Those sloping shoulders, that thick neck. Where? And then it dawned on her. This was the man who'd attacked her at the hospital.

"You aren't Billy Long."

"Bingo, bitch."

LUKE STOOD AT HIS WINDOW and watched the snowflakes drifting lazily to the ground. With the temperature dropping, the city would be blanketed in an hour or two. His gaze swung across the cul-de-sac to Keely's place. She'd turned off the foyer light, but he could see the glow of her Christmas tree in the front window. She should draw those blinds at night, he thought. Billy was in jail, but there were plenty of other violent offenders around.

Yeah, and she might consider me one of them now.

He still couldn't believe what he'd done. One minute he was in the place he most wanted to be in the world—making love to Keely. And in the next, he was a heartbeat away from forcing her. Which put him right up there—or down there—in a category with scum like Billy Long. It didn't matter that she'd been there with him until the last. When a woman said stop, a man stopped. Period. It shouldn't take tears to get his attention.

Not that tears had ever stopped his old man. He'd watched that bastard bring his mother to tears more times than he wanted to remember. Dropping the blinds, Luke moved away to pace, feeling the acid of the past burn in his belly. Was this the way it started?

And Keely had been right in everything she'd said. It was stupid and arrogant to think he could win her over with sex, no matter how good it was between them. She was too intelligent, too independent to be hustled into doing something—or agreeing to something—if she had any doubt about it.

Stopping, he squinted at the slightly tilted, childishly decorated Christmas tree and realized just how close he was to losing everything that meant anything to him. It felt as if he'd been living in limbo before Keely and Matthew had come into his life. Now he couldn't imagine going back to that lonely existence. Keely was a high-maintenance woman, all right. She'd keep him guessing and working constantly. But she was smart and sexy and opinionated and, without a doubt, the only woman in the world for him. As for Matthew, Luke cherished that little boy as if he were his real son.

Reaching up, Luke straightened the golden-haired angel on the top of the tree. So Keely wanted a man who talked. Well, that would be tough for him, but it would be a lot tougher living without her. Moving away, he headed for the fridge to get himself a beer and to figure out how to fix what he'd screwed up.

CHAPTER SIXTEEN

KEELY HELD TIGHTLY to Matthew's small hand and tried to avoid uneven places in the open playground located directly behind her apartment. Snow was now falling thickly as they made their way to a lone pickup parked near the deserted jungle gym. It was turning bitterly cold and the snow would stick, which meant that, after a few minutes, it would be difficult if not impossible to follow their path away from the complex.

Luke, please hear me. We need you now.

She'd tried every delaying tactic she could devise to stay in the apartment, hoping that Luke might come back, but in the end they'd been forced out the patio door and through the back fence. The kidnapper had bragged about accessing her yard by simply removing three of the fence boards. Now, as they left, he replaced the boards, tapping them back into place with the baseball bat. So unless anyone searching for them was particularly observant, there would be no trace of their exit.

He had, thank God, given her time to bundle Matthew up warmly and put on her down coat.

She'd brought her purse, too, but only after convincing him that her money or her ATM card might be useful.

"Where are we going?" she asked.

"My summer place," he told her with a leer. "It's fulla charm. You'll love it."

She pressed a hand against the sick feeling in her stomach and prayed for courage. Every self-defense lecture she'd ever attended emphasized the dire consequences of getting into the attacker's vehicle. Once he had his victim in a car, all the power was his.

"You can't get away with this, you know that, don't you?"

He grinned evilly as he slapped the baseball bat in the palm of his hand. "Don't look now, bitch, but I *did* get away with it."

"I'm scared, Keely," Matthew said, stumbling a little as he tried to look up at her.

Me, too. But Keely managed a smile. For Matthew's sake, she couldn't show her terror. "We're going to be okay, honey bun."

"I want Luke to go with us."

She squeezed his hand. "We'll tell him all about this when we get back," she said. *Please, God, let that be true. Let us survive to tell it.*

A curse came from the man behind them. "Don't you be whinin' for that wimp doctor, boy. You're with your real daddy now."

"You're Raymond Tucker?" Keely said, turning suddenly to look at him.

"You're not my daddy," Matthew said with surprising spirit.

"You thought it was Billy Long, eh, kid?" Tucker's mouth twisted in a sneer.

"No," Matthew said flatly. "Luke's my daddy now."

"Watch out for that hole, honey bun," Keely said, hoping to change the subject. She was afraid Matthew's loyalty to Luke might push Tucker over the edge. She hadn't decided yet whether the man was seriously deranged or just mean as a snake. Neither was a good omen for their chances to survive.

"Get a move on, both of you," Tucker said shortly. Using the baseball bat as a prod, he gave Keely a hard nudge in the small of her back, bringing sharp pain to her bruised kidneys.

"Please slow down, Mr. Tucker. If one of us twists an ankle we'll be a lot more trouble to you."

"You just let me worry about that, bitch." He swore again, obscenely. "You're gonna pay for what you did, I guess you know that, huh?"

"What did I do?"

"If you hadn't suckered my wife into hittin' the road, she wouldn't be dead now."

She turned again to look at him in confusion. "I don't know what you're talking about!"

"It's your fault Phyllis is gone and you're gonna pay!"

Matthew tugged anxiously on her hand. "I want to go home, Keely."

"Shh, sweetheart. It's okay. We'll go home soon."

"His home's with me, bitch! He never shoulda been handed over to you."

"Phyllis left Matthew with me. If you really care about him, you'll stop and consider that."

They were at the pickup now. He yanked the door open on the driver's side and shoved her inside, then roughly tossed Matthew in after her. Matthew cried out in terror. Grabbing the boy, Keely dived for the opposite door, hoping to scramble out with Matthew, but the handle had been removed.

Tucker was now behind the wheel. Muttering a furious oath, he hauled her up by her hair and slapped her hard with his open palm. Stars exploded, dazing her for a moment. She tasted blood and heard Matthew wailing.

Ignoring the boy, Tucker held her by the collar of her jacket and yelled in her face, "Do you think I'm stupid! That door's fixed so you're stuck! You got that?" He gave her a vicious shake. "You can sit here real quiet while I get us out of here or next time I hit you, it won't be with my hand. I only gave you a taste of what you needed back at the hospital.'' He nudged her chin with the baseball bat to make his point. ''Your choice, bitch.'' After getting a scared nod from her, he settled behind the wheel and made a great show of nestling the bat between his legs, then he started up the engine.

It appeared as if the bat was the only weapon he had, but to Keely it seemed almost as lethal as a gun. Tucker was a huge man. It would take only one well-placed blow to render her unconscious or worse. And then Matthew would be at his mercy. Would the man harm his own son? Or was it just Keely he planned to punish? And how? Wrapping her arms around the terrified child, Keely prayed that somehow, some way, their disappearance would be discovered before it was too late.

IT HAD TAKEN Luke about ten minutes of soul-searching to decide to go back to Keely's place and try to explain himself. He shrugged back into his jacket, closed and locked his front door and headed across the street. She couldn't have gone to bed since she hadn't yet put Oscar out to do his business; he'd been watching. He shoved his hands deep into his pockets. It was bitter cold now and the snowfall so thick that he could barely make out the traffic signal at the intersection beyond the entrance to the complex. He watched one lone pickup slow for the traffic signal, then speed up a little too much, fishtailing as it climbed the hill.

"Idiot," he muttered, noticing a couple of passengers in the pickup who didn't appear to be belted in. "Reckless idiot."

At Keely's door, he sucked in a long breath and punched the doorbell. After a moment, he backed off to get a look inside the window where the Christmas tree stood, but couldn't see movement inside. She was ticked. With reason, he thought glumly.

No sign of Oscar, either. Usually the dog was eager to greet him, jumping up on the other side of the door and barking a joyful welcome. He hit the doorbell again. And still got no response.

Could she have been foolish enough to go out at this hour? He felt a sick plunge in the pit of his stomach. Had she taken off to New Orleans without telling him? But why wouldn't she tell him? And how could she have managed to get everything together so fast? His gaze wandered to the curb. No, her car was still there and if the lights were on inside, she was just choosing to ignore him.

He fumbled in his pants pocket until he found his keys. Pulling them out, he stared at the one that fit Keely's door. If she was seriously ticked off at him, she'd be even more difficult to reason with if he used his key without permission. He punched the doorbell for the third time and when he still heard no sound of any kind, he decided to chance

it. Inserting his key, he opened the door and
stepped inside.

The first thing he noticed was the utter stillness
in the apartment. And the absence of the dog. He
called Keely's name anyway, but it echoed hol-
lowly in the silent apartment. Maybe they *had* left,
but then why hadn't he seen them? And why not
douse the lights? It was sheer stupidity to leave the
Christmas tree lit up, a fire waiting to happen. And
Keely wasn't stupid. Impetuous, yeah, rash and un-
predictable, maybe. But not stupid. With a vague
sense of unease, he stood surveying the living
room.

The fuzzy throw she'd used to cover herself lay
on the floor, but otherwise nothing seemed out of
order. Still it was not like Keely to just drop her
things on the floor.

His concern increasing, he wandered down the
hall to Matthew's room. The boy's bed was empty.
Elmo and the brown teddy lay on the floor. Idly
he picked them up. The only thing amiss was the
snow scene on the bedside table. It was tipped over
on its side. As he stood holding the stuffed animals, Luke fought an all too familiar sense of im-
pending disaster. A dank, dark cellar in Bosnia
flashed in his mind. A boy curled in a fetal position. All memories that he fought hard every day
to bury.

Wiping a hand over his face, he turned and left

Matthew's room and the bleak memories to head into Keely's bedroom. Without a light on, nothing seemed out of place, but the drapes at the patio door were open. Keely might be careless, but after the two break-ins, she did not leave drapes gaping open. He reached to click on a lamp and turned to see words scrawled in red on her mirror: *"Merry Christmas, ha-ha!"*

Heart slamming in his chest, he looked around in panic as if expecting the intruder to somehow materialize. Holding his breath, he jerked the closet door open but found it empty. Striding out of her bedroom, he inspected the bathroom, the laundry room, his apprehension growing with every footstep. The closet in Matthew's bedroom was almost an afterthought. He opened the door. Oscar lay inside, limp and still.

KEELY'S HEART SANK as Tucker exited the interstate onto what appeared to be an isolated country lane. "Where does this road lead?" she asked, mentally marking the exit.

He grinned, showing a lot of teeth. "You didn't forget, did you, sugar? We're heading for my summer place."

It was fully dark and the headlights of the pickup reflected blowing snow, thick and blinding. "It's snowing pretty hard," she said, with a worried look behind at the interstate traffic. The farther they got from the city, the more unlikely their chances of being found. "You wouldn't want to get stranded if this snowfall turns into something worse."

"You worried about me, Doctor?" he said with heavy sarcasm. "I'm touched."

"I'm worried about all of us, Mr. Tucker. A blizzard is nothing to underestimate. We've got our coats, but no boots or hats or gloves. We'd need shelter if we break down or something."

"Or something." He smirked, enjoying himself. "But you don't need to worry your pretty head. I've got it all planned. Christmas Eve is gonna be a blast!"

"I don't suppose you'd like to share the details with me," Keely said, still wondering about the man's mental state. It was hard to tell.

"No, I wouldn't want to share the details," he said, mimicking her in a singsong voice.

"We're heading for a cabin or something?" she asked.

"Or something," he repeated.

She sat silently for a moment, watching Matthew's eyes drooping sleepily. When she was satisfied that he was asleep, she asked quietly, "Wherever you're taking us, Mr. Tucker, I hope you'll keep in mind that Matthew has been through an awful lot lately. Please don't frighten him anymore."

"You stupid bitch!" She paled as he spewed forth a string of vile profanities. "You've got nerve! It's your fault he's been through a lot. If you'd kept your meddling mouth shut, Phyllis wouldn't have left and I could have talked her into coming back with me and taking the kid and we could have been happy."

"You talked to Phyllis about reconciling?"

"Hell, yeah. That bastard Long was gonna kill her. She would have been better off with me."

Keely lay a hand over Matthew's ear, praying he stayed asleep. "When was this?"

He gave her a suspicious glare. "Who wants to know?"

Keely looked straight ahead. "It's just that she didn't mention you being in the picture when she left Matthew with me. She was concerned about Billy. She knew her life was in danger and she fled for that reason." She turned her head to look at him. "I just think it's strange, her not mentioning that you were standing by to rescue her."

He literally growled, his hands flexing on the wheel. "Because you had her brainwashed, that's why!"

"I only met the woman once before she brought Matthew to me, and that was in the hospital E.R. where she was treated for a brutal battering by Billy Long. If you wanted to save her and your son, why didn't you step in before she was so desperate she felt she had to run away?''

"She wouldn't listen to me!" He took his eyes off the road to look at her. "She was running from that bastard and she'd left my boy with strangers—rank strangers, *Dr. Hamilton*—but she still wouldn't let me take care of her. You'd turned her against everybody she knew for some…some pie-in-the-sky fairy-tale life that wasn't ever going to happen!"

"You saw her after she left town?" Keely asked, pouncing on the one point in his diatribe that mattered. "You saw her while she was on the run?"

"I followed her to that goddamn motel!" he snarled. "She was my wife, not his!"

"Did you see Billy Long kill her?"

A crafty look came into his eyes. "Now why would you want to know that?"

"Because if you did, then Detective Evans would consider it valuable evidence and, if you went to him offering this evidence, he would more than likely not charge you for what you're doing now."

"You talk too much, bitch."

"I FIGURE HE'S GOT about an hour's head start, Dr. Jamison. Even if we had a clue what direction he's headed, the snow's a major deterrent." Evans drew a resigned breath. "It's a hell of a thing, Doc. If we'd had any idea her stalker wasn't Billy Long, we might have prevented this. As it is—" he was shaking his head "—I just don't know what to tell you."

Luke was pacing while trying to keep the panic inside from overflowing and ruining any chance of helping find Keely. "It's got to be that pickup I saw leaving," he said.

They'd searched the whole apartment and found nothing. But outside on the patio, they'd discovered Keely's sunglasses. Somehow, she'd managed to drop them and luckily they hadn't quite been covered by the snow. Which had led them to notice the fence. Since that was the direction from which the pickup had come, Luke figured he'd missed them by no more than five minutes.

Stopping at the huge map of the metro-Atlanta area on Evans's wall, he stared at the tiny red pin marking the location of the apartment complex and tried not to despair at the vast area surrounding it, all of which were possible routes the kidnapper had taken. Luke said to nobody in particular, "If only we knew *who* it was, we'd know *why*."

"Yeah," Detective Evans said dryly.

Oscar stood at his side, a little wobbly. The dog had some bruised ribs, but Luke had determined nothing was broken. He also had a lump on his head, which could have killed him had the blow been a little harder. If the intruder had a gun, he surely would have shot Oscar, Luke thought. The dog had been beaten, but there was no evidence of any other weapon. He was clinging to that thought. Except he knew that whoever had done this had to have used something to force Keely to leave.

One good thing, her purse was gone. And in it, she carried a cell phone. He'd tried calling her, but it was turned off. He hoped that meant she'd managed to hide it somehow. Maybe she'd get a chance to use it. It was the only hope they had.

Luke turned to look at Evans. "You think Billy Long might have an idea who did this?"

Evans shrugged. "I don't know. We can ask him."

"He's denied all along that he killed Phyllis," Luke said. "So if he didn't, who else would have a motive?"

"We've been down that road," Evans said, rising from his chair. "It's a dead end. She had no known enemies, no other lovers. Actually, she didn't even have any friends. The woman was totally isolated from anybody but Billy."

"Typical for battered women," Luke said. He knew a lot more about domestic abuse now, thanks to Keely. Phyllis, unfortunately, was only one in thousands, tens of thousands.

"Her ex-husband never turned up, did he?" Luke asked.

"No, we have his parole officer alerted, however."

"I wonder if Billy knows him." He glanced at Evans. "I think we should pay him a visit."

Evans nodded. "Let's do it."

BILLY LONG WAS FEELING sullen and mistreated. He'd been in jail just long enough to convince himself that he was a victim of an unfair justice system and not quite long enough to fully realize the seriousness of the charges against him. Suspicion of murder was bogus. He kept telling the dumb asses who'd arrested him that he hadn't killed Phyllis, but so far his court-appointed attorney—another dumb ass—hadn't managed to spring him. No big deal. He made up his mind early on that he'd cop to the breaking-and-entering at the doctor's apartment, which he'd done only once, no matter what they said, but he didn't kill Phyllis and he wasn't going to go down for it.

"You got a visitor, Long."

Billy stood up as the deputy unlocked the cell. "Who is it? My lawyer?"

"I'm not a butler, Long. And you don't get calling cards here. You'll know who it is when you get out there."

It was that black detective, Evans or something, and the tough doctor. Things were looking up, Billy thought as he went inside the interrogation room and sat down where the deputy pointed. "What's up?" he asked as soon as the cuffs were removed. "Y'all ready to let an innocent man go?"

"If we had an innocent man," Evans replied.

The big detective sat across from Long at the steel table while the doctor remained standing. He looked like hell, Billy thought, noting the strain around the eyes and the tight line of the mouth. Billy remembered him from that night in the hospital and decided he wasn't the kind of man he wanted to piss off.

He spread his hands, happy to be uncuffed. "How can I help you, gentlemen?"

"Somebody broke into Keely Hamilton's apartment, Billy," Evans said softly. "Dr. Hamilton and Matthew have been kidnapped."

"No shit!" Billy breathed with genuine astonishment.

"We thought you might know something."

"How could I know anything locked up in here this way?"

"You admitted one count of breaking into Dr. Hamilton's place. If that's true, then someone else was stalking her, too. If you have any information you'd like to share to shed some light on this other creep, now's the time to speak up."

Billy rubbed his fingers over his beard thoughtfully. "What about the charge against me?"

"Suspicion of murder? Cooperate fully and it'll be easier on you, that's all I can promise."

"Not that charge!" Billy said irritably. "I didn't kill Phyllis. I've told you that over and over. You got no evidence, so it's just a matter of time until that jerko appointed by the court gets me out of here. I'm talking the B and E charge at the doc's place."

"Breaking and entering," Evans said, leaning back. "That's something else. Give us something, it's wiped out."

"Maybe you ought to look at her husband," Billy said. It was a shot in the dark. He didn't know a damn thing about Phyllis's ex, but hell, Tucker could be bent out of shape over her refusing to let him see the kid.

Luke turned, eyeing him sharply. "Raymond Tucker?"

"Yeah, that's him. He made noises all the time about wanting the kid, but he's an ex-con and Phyllis didn't trust him."

"And she trusted you?" Evans remarked.

"She did, yeah." Billy drew himself up, looking offended. "I worked every day, man. I brought my paychecks home. I paid the rent, kept my vehicle in top shape, we ate out…a lot. I was a good provider."

"Yeah, Billy, you're a real catch for a woman." Evans began to write in his notebook. "What can you tell us about Tucker? Where does he hang out?''

"Hell, I don't know! I'm just saying he had a thing for Phyllis and he wanted the kid. But she wouldn't see him, so when he got out of the clink this time, she told his parole officer not to give him her address.''

Luke drove a frustrated hand through his hair. "Is Tucker capable of violence? Did he ever threaten her?''

"You want my opinion, he's capable of anything," Billy said. Beneath the table, his knees bumped as he shifted in the chair.

Luke paced to the barred window and back again. "Can you think of any place he might have taken Keely and the boy...if he's the kidnapper?''

"Actually, now that I think about it..." Billy straightened up as if actually giving the matter some thought. "There was a hunting cabin Tucker used to like in the woods a little south of here. Said it belonged to a relative of his. We drove out to it once, me and Phyllis, but it didn't look like a place I'd want to spend any time in. If it's him who's kidnapped them, you might want to check it out.''

THE CABIN WAS HARDLY A CHARMER, but Tucker had apparently made preparations for an extended stay. He'd stocked cans of food, coffee, rice, dried beans and jugs of bottled water. There was also a pile of cut wood for the potbellied stove, the only source of heat in the cabin. After watching Keely place Matthew, still sleeping, on a cot and tucking him in with a blanket, which he'd also provided, Tucker had forced her to sit while he stoked a fire in the stove.

She still didn't know whether he just wanted to stake his claim to Matthew, had brought her along to temporarily allay Matthew's fear and would get rid of her as soon as her usefulness was over, or if he had another plan. What worried her most was his admission that he'd followed Phyllis to the motel where she'd been murdered. Billy Long had denied any involvement in Phyllis's death. Could he have been telling the truth? Was Tucker the murderer?

"I could use a cup of coffee," she told him, seeking anything to distract him from whatever he planned after he got the fire going.

"Then make it."

Glad to be doing something, she got up and began assembling what she needed to brew coffee. She'd shoved her purse beneath the blanket where Matthew slept, praying Tucker wouldn't think to examine it. Although when she might get an opportunity to use the cell phone was doubtful so long as he insisted on watching her every minute. But sooner or later she would have to use the bathroom. If, that is, there was a bathroom. Somehow she'd try to smuggle it in there.

And what if there was no signal out here? She wasn't certain how cell phones worked in rural areas and hoped they weren't too deep in the woods to get a call through. She calculated they'd been on that country road only a few miles, four at most. If she could find a signal, the cell phone offered the best chance for rescue. With the snow falling like this, and no trail to follow or way to suggest that Raymond Tucker was her stalker, she couldn't rely on anybody but herself to get her and Matthew out of here.

She found the coffeepot inside the only cabinet and uncapped a jug to fill it with water. She'd been in hot spots before, mostly as a rebellious teenager on the streets. She'd survived that. She'd survive this, she vowed, and so would Matthew. Her mind made up, she reached for the coffee.

"WE COULD BE THERE inside thirty minutes if it wasn't for this damned snowstorm," Evans muttered, hunched over the wheel of a big Ford Expedition. It was the largest vehicle on hand at the station as they'd prepared to head out to look for Tucker's cabin. It was also fitted with snow tires.

Beside him, Luke worked to contain his frustration and fear. If anything happened to Keely and Matthew, he didn't think he could survive it. Marriage or not, he was committed to them both in all the ways that counted. He'd been a fool to think he could avoid the pain of commitment simply by not recognizing it.

"You get us out to that exit off the interstate and I'll find the friggin' cabin," Billy Long said from the back seat.

Luke could see that Billy was enjoying himself. A few hours ago, it would have been inconceivable that he would be tooling along the interstate playing a role in the rescue of his stepson and Keely, who'd been the catalyst for his troubles. Evans, of course, had insisted on the handcuffs and a large deputy to keep him in line. Cuffed or not, Luke figured Billy preferred this excursion to spending time in jail.

"I told Phyllis all along that her ex was one mean dude," Billy said, squinting to find landmarks in the driving snow. "And if it turns out that he's the one who killed her, I hope you guys let me take a shot at him."

Luke and Detective Evans exchanged a look. "I'd think twice before trying anything, if I were you," Evans said. "You're here to show us where the cabin is. If Tucker is the kidnapper, the justice system will handle his punishment."

"I really loved that woman," Billy said after a moment, still gazing out at the snow. "Only time we ever had words was when I had a little too much to drink.'' He was shaking his head. ''Phyllis just didn't have any patience with booze.''

Evans grunted. Luke stared stonily ahead.

''We're close to the exit,'' Billy said, suddenly perking up. ''Won't be long now.''

CHAPTER SEVENTEEN

"I NEED TO GO TO THE BATHROOM, Keely."

Keely set the coffeepot on top of the hot stove and nervously wiped her hands down the sides of her jeans. This might be her only chance. "Where's the bathroom, Mr. Tucker?"

"Where do you think? This ain't the Holiday Inn."

"Where exactly is it?" she asked the man.

"Outside. Tell him to hold it. Be a man."

"He's a little boy, Mr. Tucker. A four-year-old needs to go potty frequently. If he has an accident, his clothes will be wet, and we don't have a change for him, if you recall."

"You're just full of talk, aren't you, bitch?"

"I'm only being reasonable."

"Meaning I'm unreasonable?" He slammed the baseball bat against the stove, rattling the coffee-pot, which splattered on the hot surface, sizzling and hissing.

"Just tell me where the facilities are and I'll take Matthew. What can it matter? We can't go any-where. It's snowing."

"You got a smart mouth, you know that?" Then he grunted, accepting the logic of a four-year-old's needs. But not before kicking at a log that was stacked nearby to feed the fire. "There's a lean-to just outside the backdoor. Be back in two minutes."

Keely went over to the cot and sat down beside Matthew. Her injured hand might hamper her, but she had to try. Slipping one arm around him, she made a big show of bundling him in the blanket while she took the cell phone from her purse.

"It'll be cold out there," she said, before he questioned the need for taking the blanket.

"Yeah, it'll be cold," he mocked with a twist of his mouth.

She stood up, securing the cell phone in the folds of the blanket by lifting Matthew.

"I can walk, Keely," he said, wiggling to get down.

"I know, honey bun, but you might trip over the blanket. I'll put you down in a jiffy."

"It better be a jiffy," Tucker said, following them to the door. "I want the kid to go back to sleep because I got plans for you, sugar."

After he'd started the fire to warm the place up, Keely had noticed Tucker becoming more and more agitated. She wasn't sure what his problem was. Maybe he was having second thoughts about his rashness in kidnapping them, or maybe he was worried that the cabin was a bad choice. Who knows what he was thinking. Or planning. If he killed her—as she now suspected he'd killed Phyllis—he must know he'd eventually be a suspect. But she couldn't afford to dwell on that just now. First, she had to try and figure out a way to escape.

She stepped outside, holding Matthew close. Before they'd taken two steps, she almost lost her breath in the cold, blowing wind and snow. Fortunately, the lean-to was attached to the main building and accessible after walking only a few feet. She was glad to see it had a sturdy door. Forced to set Matthew down, she struggled to open it and finally managed to get them both inside. Instantly she locked it with a simple hook, knowing it would hold only a second or two if Tucker wanted to get at them. She had no time to lose.

"It's cold in here, Keely," Matthew said, his eyes big and scared.

"I know, sweetie." She whipped the blanket off and helped him with his clothes. It was too cold to remove his jacket.

Matthew stared at the primitive facilities. "Are you sure this is a bathroom, Keely?"

Under any other circumstances, Keely would have laughed. But not now. "It's old-fashioned, Matthew, and I'll show you how in just a minute, but first I need to make a phone call."

"You're gonna call Luke?"

"I'm going to try. And Detective Evans."

"That's a good idea."

"Yeah, I think so." She quickly punched the power button and watched as the roam signal was displayed. *Hallelujah!* There was a signal. She'd already decided on 9-1-1 first instead of Luke's number. He could have discovered them missing and then wouldn't be in his apartment to answer. She quickly checked through a crack in the boards of the lean-to before dialing, but there was no sign of Tucker. She dialed the emergency three-digit code.

A voice crackling and breaking up answered. Keely plunged right in. "Hello, this is Dr. Keely Hamilton. This is an emergency. Please—"

"Where are…" crackle, crackle "…calling…from?"

"Listen! I don't have much time. I've been kidnapped by a man named Raymond Tucker. I'm at a cabin off the interstate. The exit is—"

"You're…" more static "…up…bad connection…"

"Did you get anything I said?" Keely cried. She was terrified the woman would fade out and any chance of getting through again would be lost.

"…cabin…interstate…if you…landmarks for police…"

"Exit at MacDonald Road," she said, speaking as forcefully as she dared. "Drive about four miles to a sign that advertises land for sale. It's on the right. Turn there.''

"Would...repeat that?''

Keely took a desperate breath. "MacDonald Road, four miles to a sign advertising land. Turn right.''

Crackle...more static...crackle. "...on the way... stay on the line.''

"I can't stay on the line,'' Keely wailed, almost panicking as the cabin door suddenly opened. She quickly thrust the phone into her coat pocket without breaking the connection. Maybe it would help, maybe not.

She jumped as Tucker banged on the door with the baseball bat and Matthew whimpered. "Time's up! Come outta there!''

"We need another minute, Mr. Tucker,'' she said, helping Matthew sit down on the primitive seat. "Matthew had to take a minute to get used to the unfamiliar facilities.''

"Kid's a wimp,'' Tucker grumbled. "Spent too much time with Phyllis pandering to him. Spoiled him rotten. But I'm gonna fix that.''

"Not if I can help it,'' Keely vowed softly, one arm wrapped protectively around the little boy, waiting for him to finish.

"I want to go home, Keely,'' he said in a small voice. It hurt her that he was being subjected to yet another traumatic incident when he'd been forced to bear so much already. If they should get out of this, how would this child ever overcome all he'd seen in his first four years?

She lifted him up and helped him fix his clothes. "We're going home, darling," she told him, kissing the top of his head. "I promise. Please be a brave boy. Luke's coming for us soon." Then, wrapping him again in the blanket, she opened the door of the lean-to. Tucker waited, clad in a thick down jacket, holding the baseball bat. She stepped around him, ignoring the sharp jab he gave her, and hurried back into the cabin.

The first thing she noticed after settling Matthew once again on the cot was that Tucker seemed less agitated. He sat in a kitchen chair near the glowing stove, his feet stuck out and his hands resting on his belt. He'd shed his jacket and the baseball bat actually lay on the floor.

Keely made a great show of pouring herself a cup of coffee and one for Tucker. She then headed across to him, setting his cup on a rickety apple crate upended near his chair. "Coffee's ready," she said.

He glanced up and she saw immediately that his pupils were dilated and that he was having trouble focusing. She remembered Evans saying that he'd been jailed on a drug charge.

"Coffee." He repeated the word as if she'd suggested milk. "Hey, babe, I've got something a lot better than coffee."

She was "babe" now, not "bitch." Clearly he was high on something. He must have waited for them to go to the outhouse before shooting up. Or snorting. Whatever. She shuddered at the thought of what effect the drugs might have on a man like Raymond Tucker. Would he be less hostile, more hostile? Unchanged?

He managed a drunken smile. "Wanna join me?"

"No, thanks."

His smile vanished. "Just like Phyllis. She never liked the good stuff, either."

"Was that the reason she wanted the divorce?"

"It's what she *said*," he replied, rubbing his nose before resettling in an even more horizontal position. "But what she *meant* was that she'd found somebody else." He paused so long that Keely thought he might have passed out. But then he added, "It was Phyllis…set the cops on me, did you know that?"

"No."

"I waited…to get out…to get my revenge." His words were slurred now, barely understandable. Whatever he'd taken, it had been a heavy hit; she recognized the signs and blessed her E.R. experience with junkies. In a few more minutes, he would be almost comatose. Elated, she hid her expression as she sipped her coffee. Depending on the amount he'd taken, he just might have handed her and Matthew their chance to escape.

Keely glanced back to see whether Matthew was listening. Wrapped in the blanket, he had his thumb in his mouth and was curled up in a ball, having trouble keeping his eyes open.

"Revenge?" she repeated, turning her gaze back to Tucker.

"What?" he said, frowning blearily.

"You mentioned getting revenge on Phyllis."

"Oh, yeah." He frowned, trying to concentrate. "I had a plan."

"What was your plan?"

Another fatuous grin. "I…waited until she left that…jerk…and I followed her." Suddenly he seemed to realize he was losing his grip. He blinked a few times, rubbed both hands over his face and made a halfhearted effort to straighten up. But after a moment or two, he settled back with a sigh. "It was easy to get inside the…motel room. Stupid broad…she let me in on the first try."

"And you killed her."

"Yeah." How could a man look evil and sly even when zonked out of his mind on drugs? But Raymond Tucker managed it. He smiled at her. "Just like I'm gonna kill you."

TRAFFIC ON THE INTERSTATE had slowed to a crawl for the few determined drivers who refused to wait out the storm. Evans was driving as fast as he dared in the hazardous conditions, but it wasn't fast enough for Luke.

"Speed it up, can't you?" Luke was hunched forward, trying to see any landmark in the snowy world outside.

"And wind up like this guy?" Evans swerved to miss an eighteen-wheeler cocked sideways across the six-lane freeway. "We're making good time, considering. We don't want to screw up now."

Luke took a deep breath. All his thoughts were fixed on the woman he loved and the boy who would be his son. He was stunned at the depth of emotion he felt. It was as though he'd spent the past few years in an emotional vacuum and now all the love and pain and fear bottled up inside him was threatening to break through and overwhelm him.

He twisted to look behind him at Billy Long. "Are you certain about the exit?"

"Yeah, it's MacDonald Road. Keep your eyes peeled. We're nearly there."

Everyone tensed when the radio squawked. "That's my call sign," Evans said, reaching for the mouthpiece.

A distress 9-1-1 had been received from Dr. Keely Hamilton, Evans was told. She was in a cabin somewhere on the interstate, but the operator had not been able to understand the exact location. They'd notify Evans if she called back, but so far no other call had come in.

"Hot damn!" Billy said gleefully. "We're on the right track! Didn't I tell you? Hold on, Doc, the cavalry's on the way!"

Luke wanted to choke that stupid grin off his face, but they still needed him to find the cabin. Afterward, he promised himself. Afterward, he'd take a strip off his redneck hide. "There might have been no need for a rescue if you'd told Detective Evans what you knew about Raymond Tucker in the first place," Luke said.

"Hey, I'm just an innocent bystander in all this," Billy said, looking wounded. "It was you guys who couldn't put it all together till it was too late."

Grinding his teeth, Luke rubbed a hand over his face and discovered in spite of the cold that he was sweating with fear. He thought of Randall Barlow and his reliance on faith and prayer. If ever both were needed, now was the time. He turned around then and faced the road...just in time to see the green sign for the MacDonald Road exit materialize out of the snow.

To KILL HER, he'd have to sober up first. Keely sat still and silent for the next few minutes, waiting for the drug to work its magic on Raymond Tucker's brain. She needed the keys to his pickup, but if she couldn't get them without alerting him, she'd simply have to move to Plan B. She looked at Matthew, relieved that he was sleeping again. When she carried him out of the cabin, he would need to be quiet as a mouse. Maybe, if fate was kind, this whole episode would just seem like a nightmare to him.

Meanwhile, she waited in a fever of impatience. The only sound was the soft hiss from the coffee-pot as it boiled on the too-hot stove. Had the 9-1-1 dispatcher deciphered enough of the call to send help? Had Luke been notified? Her gaze moved to the door of the cabin. Was he on his way? She'd always prided herself on her indepen-dence, but she freely admitted she'd love to see Luke walk through that door just now. It amazed her how much he'd come to mean to her in the time their lives had become entangled.

But it seemed as if this was one predicament she'd have to manage alone.

Holding her breath, she got to her feet quietly. In the stark silence of the room, even the silken rustle of her down coat seemed too loud. Tucker, however, did not stir. Not a hair.

Could she risk trying to get the keys? What if they weren't in his coat pocket, but in his pants? She decided not to even attempt searching his pockets. If the door was unlocked she'd hot-wire the pickup. And if it was locked, she'd break the window. Those wild teenage years were finally going to be put to good use.

Keeping one eye on Tucker, she moved silently across the room to check the door. It wouldn't matter how clever her escape plan if they couldn't get out of the cabin itself. But luck was with her. The door only had a dead bolt. Glancing once more at Tucker, she turned it and heard the click with a scared jump of her heart. Still no reaction from Tucker. She'd seen junkies like him. If Evans was right, his drug of choice was cocaine and he'd taken a big hit as soon as he had a moment alone. Depending on its purity, he might be incapacitated for hours. Why he'd been so reckless, when he was on a crime spree with two hostages, only Tucker himself could know.

Unwilling to actually open the door, she went over to Matthew and tucked the blanket snugly around him before slipping her arm beneath him to hoist him onto her shoulder. He made a snuffling, sleeping-child sound and she kissed his ear, whispering soothing words. She breathed with relief as he settled quietly on her shoulder. Then, despite the little boy's deadweight, she crept across the floor and managed finally to get the door open.

Once down the porch steps, Keely hightailed it to the truck. Matthew was stirring now. She reluctantly stood him against the pickup while she held her breath and tried the door, fumbling a bit because of her sprained finger. Unlocked, as she'd hoped! The possibility that she'd try to leave in his pickup had apparently never occurred to Tucker.

Quickly she bundled Matthew inside, jumped in herself, closed the door as quietly as possible and sat for a moment breathing a prayer. Digging in her purse, she found a tiny penlight. Then, rubbing her hands together, she bent down and reached beneath the steering wheel of the aging pickup in search of the right wires.

"Whatcha doin', Keely?"

"A little magic trick, honey bun." Using the penlight, she sorted through a maze of wires and finally found the two that she needed to spark the ignition. She hoped. It had been a few years. "Some things you never forget," she murmured with satisfaction as the starter kicked and the truck jumped. Oops, she'd forgotten to take it out of gear.

"You better hurry, Keely," the little boy advised a moment later, "'cause that man just opened the door."

"Oh, no."

Her heart swelled with the sweet sound of the motor just as Raymond Tucker stumbled off the porch, waving the baseball bat. She last saw him as she gunned the pickup, fishtailing briefly, and sped off down the country lane.

"WHAT THE HELL!" Evans braked hard, blinded by the headlights of a vehicle careening around the curve in front of him. The big Expedition slid sideways and almost veered off into a ditch. Coming to a stop at the same time as the oncoming driver, Evans hesitated just long enough to catch a breath and grab Luke, who had his door open, ready to charge.

"Hold it! Let me check this out before you go flying off half-cocked."

But Luke was beyond caution. He saw the door of the pickup open and Keely's head appeared. "That's Keely." He was out, slogging through the snow toward her before Evans managed to pull his weapon out. With a soft cry, Keely flew into Luke's arms and was lifted off the ground into a crushing embrace. For a few seconds, they simply stood locked together, savoring the sweetness of a narrow escape.

"Luke, Luke, I was so scared," she told him, breathing the words against the warmth of his throat.

"Me, too." He held her close while he searched over her head for Matthew. "Is Matthew okay?" But he saw the boy just then, tumbling out of the pickup in a tangle of blanket and short legs and sneakers. Kicking free, he started toward them in the snow, keeping to the trail made by Keely.

"I want to go home, Luke!" he said, arms lifted.

Luke swept him up, swallowing hard on a wave of love, and enfolded him into the hug with Keely. "That's where we're headed, son," he said huskily.

"Me and Keely were really scared," Matthew said, snuggling close to Luke. "That man hurted Oscar and threw him in a closet and I was afraid he would hurt us, too."

"You're a brave boy," Luke said, feeling the small arms almost choking him and wondering why a biological father would subject his own flesh and blood to such an ordeal. "And Oscar's okay. I let him out of that closet and he only has a little bump."

Pulling back, Matthew looked into Luke's face. "Keely saved us with that phone you made her keep in her purse."

"It was a miracle that I even found a signal," Keely said. "And then when I did dial 9-1-1, the dispatcher kept asking me to repeat everything. The whole time I was trying to keep my voice down so Tucker wouldn't hear me, or worse, come out there where we were." She made a face. "I shouldn't have worried, he had other things on his mind."

"Like what?"

"Like getting high."

Luke nodded slowly. "That's how you managed to sneak away and get the pickup."

"Yes."

"She didn't even have the keys! So she used a magic trick!" Matthew said, wiggling to get down and resume his big-boy persona now that he was safe and reunited with the two people he loved most.

Setting him on his feet, Luke straightened up and asked, "What kind of magic trick?"

"I hot-wired the ignition," Keely said.

"I didn't hear that, Doc!" Evans said in passing, on his way to inspect the interior of the pickup.

"Hot-wired the ignition?" Luke repeated. "How—"

She spread her hands and said sheepishly, "I told you I had a colorful past."

Beyond laughing, he caught her up again and swung her around. Then as he slowly set her on her feet, he looked in her eyes. "Will you please marry me, Keely?"

She put out a hand and tenderly brushed snow from his hair. "Yes."

"I have things to tell you."

She kept her eyes locked on his, searching for something that—at last—she saw there. "All right."

"I love you. I loved you all along, but I just didn't know it."

She nodded. "I love you, too."

"We'll adopt Matthew, okay?"

"Of course." Then her face changed. "Oh! There's something I need to tell Detective Evans!" She turned as Evans was closing the door of the pickup. In his hand he held a small plastic bag with a green-brown substance in it.

"Weed," he said shortly. Then, surveying Keely and Matthew with a policeman's eye, he asked, "You and the boy okay, Doc?"

"Yes, we're fine, but never mind that just now. Raymond killed Phyllis. It wasn't Billy Long."

"Did he tell you that?"

"Yes, he admitted it."

Evans nodded and seemed unsurprised. "After this caper, I was thinking he might be the killer."

"He's at the cabin, but he's so disoriented that I don't think he'll be any trouble to arrest."

"Disoriented," Luke repeated with a skeptical look. "On marijuana?"

"No, cocaine," she said, rolling her eyes. "He stupidly decided to go for a hit, so I waited until he'd passed out, then I gathered Matthew and my things together and we left."

"Just like that," Luke said, "you left."

"More or less," Keely said.

Matthew, tired of waiting, tugged hard at Luke's jeans. "Can we go home now?"

"You bet, son." More than ready to have Keely to himself, Luke caught the boy's hand and slipped his other arm around her. As they headed toward the police vehicle, the deputy got out with his handcuffed prisoner. Luke felt Matthew latch onto his leg in fear. He picked him up and the little boy's arms went around his neck in terror. "It's okay, son," he murmured. "You're safe now. Nobody's going to hurt you again."

Keely stared as the man raised his cuffed hands and waved at her. "Is that Billy Long?"

"He's the only one who knew the location of the cabin. Evans has radioed for more manpower and a couple more vehicles, so we won't have to ride back with him."

"Good, because I don't want him within a mile of Matthew. And I hope he doesn't expect me to thank him."

"No, he plea-bargained with Evans. That's thanks enough."

KEELY CAME OUT of her bedroom after taking a long shower in an attempt to wash away the stench of the cabin and the terror of the experience. Thankfully Matthew had gone willingly to bed after he saw for himself that Oscar was okay and Luke and Keely had promised to be in the apartment when he woke up in the morning. She didn't know what lasting damage had been done by the experience and she prayed for wisdom and insight in the future. She and Luke had discussed on the way home that if some therapy was needed, they would gladly cooperate. The important thing was that they were sure to be offered the chance to adopt Matthew.

She poured herself a glass of wine as Luke finished a phone call. "Who was that?" she asked.

"Your father."

"My father," she said softly, smiling. "That has a nice sound, doesn't it?"

"Yeah. I called Laura and Randall to let them know what happened. They said to tell you they hoped you'd come over Christmas morning. They want this particular holiday to be special. You're family now and if you're not going to New Orleans, they'd like you to spend it with them."

"Me and Matthew?" she asked, her heart beating fast.

"And me. My mother will be coming, too."

She smiled. "Nice." Then, after hesitating, "Was it just my father, or is this Laura's idea, too?"

"Laura wanted me to make certain you knew the invitation was from both of them."

Keely felt quick tears start in her eyes. "That's just...so wonderful, isn't it, Luke?"

"Yeah. Maybe it took another near-tragedy to break through Laura's grief. She was shocked to learn that you're Randall's daughter, anybody would be. But I think she was already softening toward you before she was told."

"We have Matthew to thank for that," Keely said.

"Yeah." He watched her bend down and pick up Matthew's sneakers and place them neatly on a stack of other things to be taken to his room. "Come here."

He held out his hand and she took it. He drew her into his arms and sat down on the couch, settling her on his lap. She leaned over and set her wineglass on the coffee table, drawing a groan from him as she locked her arms around his neck. "This has a familiar feel," she said, kissing the underside of his jaw.

He framed her face with his hands, forcing her to look into his eyes. "I've been doing a lot of thinking lately, Keely," he said quietly. "And I've been wrong about a lot of things. I should have told you what happened that turned me against a career in the military. I should have explained about my dad and my fear that I'd be as rotten a father as he was. And then today when I almost lost control and you were saying no—"

"Stop." Keely put a finger on his mouth, his beautiful, sensual mouth. "*We* almost lost control,

Luke. Both of us. Don't you think I was just as aroused as you? And you did stop. When I asked you to.''

"For a minute, I felt too much like my old man.''

"Why?''

"My old man communicated with a slap and a hard word. He was a hard-ass who expected the house to be run like a military base and my mother to be the first sergeant. Note that she wasn't to be accorded officer status,'' he added bitterly. "The way he treated her, she could have been a buck private. I watched all the joy drain out of her, all the self-confidence. I watched my younger brother turn to drugs. With that kind of background, how could I get married and have kids?''

She looked at him sitting there stiff as a general, his features stern as his father's must have been, but his eyes...oh, his eyes. He couldn't hide the turmoil and pain in those wonderful eyes. And her heart turned over. He was nothing like his father. Laura had been right. He was decent and honorable and honest and brave. He was also opinionated and close minded and stubborn. He'd be hell to live with sometimes, but other times...oh, he was going to be worth the trouble.

She sought to find the right words. "Seems to me that you know all the wrong things a husband

and father does, Luke. I'd like to think that would go a long way to helping you do the job properly.''

''I thought it would be easier and safer to hold myself back,'' he said, stroking her hair behind an ear. ''But I just kept needing you more. I was lonely when you weren't around. I'd never been lonely before.''

''Me neither.''

The air went out of his lungs at her reply. ''I never would have guessed that. You don't…didn't seem to need anyone.''

''I need you and Matthew. I always did.''

''Matthew.'' He settled his hands at her waist. ''I need to explain about Matthew and…and why I felt reluctant taking on the responsibility of a little kid.''

She said nothing, waiting for him to go on.

''A twelve-year-old boy died because of a decision I made on an assignment in Bosnia.''

''I'm so sorry,'' she said, knowing how devastating the loss of any patient was to Luke. How much more agonizing that he felt personally responsible for this boy's death.

''I left the Army after that.''

''And went into medical school.''

''Yeah.''

''Good choice.'' Unable to keep her hands off him, she cradled his jaw in one hand and made him look at her. ''But I can never accept that you

caused a child's death. Circumstances may have
brought about a tragedy, but Bosnia was a country
torn apart by war, Luke. Terrible things happen in
wartime.''

''Yeah.'' Luke had heard all of that before and
it had never helped. But to his amazement, he realized he was ready to accept it now. He wasn't
sure how that had happened, but he wasn't willing
to dwell on it at this moment. Instead, he was wishing they were in the bedroom, in bed. He wanted
to reaffirm his claim on the woman sitting on his
lap and driving him crazy. He wanted to hear her
tell him again that she loved him. He wanted to
show her how much he loved her and he planned
on taking what was left of the night to do it. And
then he'd try to tell her in words. He knew she'd
want that.

''Luke?''

''What?''

She smiled a wry smile. ''All out of words, Dr.
Jamison?''

His heart was pounding at the base of his throat.
A man could change only so much in a short time.
''Would you take it wrong if I were to do this?''
He stood up abruptly, keeping an arm beneath her
bottom so that, with a squeal, she had to curl her
legs around his waist.

''Oh, hell! Did I hurt you? I keep forgetting
you're bruised all over.''

"Not all over," she said, hanging on when he tried to set her back on her feet. "Where are we going?" she asked, pressing a kiss to a spot on his neck that she knew drove him crazy.

"Bed. We're going to bed. But we'll talk more…after."

"Is that a promise?" she asked, clinging close to keep from bumping into the door frame as he maneuvered them into her bedroom and straight to the bed.

"It's a promise." He lay her down and then followed, liking the feel of her beneath him. Desire rose in him like a fountain and he bent to kiss her. Just before their lips met, she smiled, her eyes every bit as bright as the sparkling lights she'd strung in her Christmas tree. In the hall, he heard her clock strike midnight. Christmas Eve.

"Merry Christmas," she whispered.

SILHOUETTE®
SUPERROMANCE™

AVAILABLE FROM 20TH DECEMBER 2002

THE CALAMITY JANES Sherryl Woods

Calamity Janes

Emma Rogers's oldest friends were urging her to look with favour on her sexy nemesis, Ford Hamilton! Even her daughter sang the praises of the man she'd clashed with on a controversial court case. How could she resist his offer to match wits—and join hearts—with him for a lifetime?

SIDE EFFECTS Bobby Hutchinson

Emergency!

Dr Alexandra Ross loves her job in the hectic emergency department. But she also loves her husband, Sergeant Cameron Ross. Then Cam is suddenly transferred to a sleepy little town to save his life. Can Alex ever accept a new kind of medicine—and a new kind of husband?

LUKE'S DAUGHTERS Lynnette Kent

The Brennan Brothers

Luke Brennan meets Sarah Randolph on the worst day of his life—his brother's wedding day. Presumed dead for six years, Luke's brother has returned to reclaim the family Luke had made his own. Now only Sarah knows how much he hurts. And only she can begin to fill the emptiness in his heart. If he'll let her...

ARE YOU MY MUMMY? Kay David

Count on a Cop

Abbie Franklin is approached by a lost little boy and has no choice but to help him—even though that means dealing with her ex-husband, policeman Ray Menendez. *He* knows the sensible thing would be to hand the child over to the proper authorities—but the sensible thing isn't always the right thing...

AVAILABLE FROM 20TH DECEMBER 2002

SILHOUETTE®

Sensation™

Passionate, dramatic, thrilling romances

HIS FATHER'S SON Ruth Langan
THE MAN WHO WOULD BE KING Linda Turner
THE TRUTH ABOUT TOBY Cheryl St. John
REMEMBER THE NIGHT Linda Castillo
BEAUTY AND THE BADGE Lyn Stone
KEEPING CAROLINE Vickie Taylor

Special Edition™

Vivid, satisfying romances full of family, life and love

SINGLE WITH TWINS Joan Elliott Pickart
THE GROOM'S STAND-IN Gina Wilkins
IN LOVE WITH HER BOSS Christie Ridgway
ANOTHER MAN'S CHILDREN Christine Flynn
THE CHILD SHE ALWAYS WANTED Jennifer Mikels
ON PINS AND NEEDLES Victoria Pade

Intrigue™

Danger, deception and suspense

A WOMAN WITH A MYSTERY BJ Daniels
SCARLET VOWS Dani Sinclair
STATE OF EMERGENCY Cassie Miles
MIDNIGHT BURNING Caroline Burnes

Desire™ 2 in 1

Two intense, sensual love stories in one volume

THE PLAYBOY SHEIKH Alexandra Sellers
BILLIONAIRE BACHELORS: STONE Anne Marie Winston

TAMING BLACKHAWK Barbara McCauley
MICHAEL'S TEMPTATION Eileen Wilks

NAVY SEAL DAD Metsy Hingle
DR DESIRABLE Kristi Gold

SILHOUETTE® SUPERROMANCE™

Popular author
Bobby Hutchinson
is delighted to offer you

EMERGENCY!

*If you love the emotional suspense and
the drama of all the television medical
shows, then this is the series for you.
Set your heart pounding with…*

SIDE EFFECTS
January 2003

THE BABY DOCTOR
April 2003

FALLING FOR THE DOCTOR
July 2003

FREE

2 BOOKS
AND A SURPRISE GIFT!

We would like to take this opportunity to thank you for reading this Silhouette® book by offering you the chance to take TWO more specially selected titles from the Superromance™ series absolutely FREE! We're also making this offer to introduce you to the benefits of the Reader Service™—

- ★ FREE home delivery
- ★ FREE monthly Newsletter
- ★ FREE gifts and competitions
- ★ Exclusive Reader Service discount
- ★ Books available before they're in the shops

Accepting these FREE books and gift places you under no obligation to buy; you may cancel at any time, even after receiving your free shipment. Simply complete your details below and return the entire page to the address below. *You don't even need a stamp!*

YES! Please send me 2 free Superromance books and a surprise gift. I understand that unless you hear from me, I will receive 4 superb new titles every month for just £3.49 each, postage and packing free. I am under no obligation to purchase any books and may cancel my subscription at any time. The free books and gift will be mine to keep in any case.

U2ZEC

Ms/Mrs/Miss/Mr ....Initials................................

BLOCK CAPITALS PLEASE

Surname...

Address..

....

....Postcode ....

Send this whole page to:
UK: FREEPOST CN81, Croydon, CR9 3WZ
EIRE: PO Box 4546, Kilcock, County Kildare (stamp required)

Offer valid in UK and Eire only and not available to current Reader Service subscribers to this series. We reserve the right to refuse an application and applicants must be aged 18 years or over. Only one application per household. Terms and prices subject to change without notice. Offer expires 31st March 2003. As a result of this application, you may receive offers from Harlequin Mills & Boon and other carefully selected companies. If you would prefer not to share in this opportunity please write to The Data Manager at the address above.

Silhouette® is a registered trademark used under licence.
Superromance™ is being used as a trademark.